Death in the Valley

I0566563

A Trio of Award-Winning
Mystery Shorts
by Susan Tuttle

These stories were written specifically for the Dead Bird Competition, the annual writer's contest of the San Joaquin Chapter of Sisters in Crime (SinC).

The Telltale Death won the Baby Bird award in 2008 (best story by a first time entrant)
Beef Killington won third place and Best Use of Setting in 2009
Hydro-Synth won second place and the Most Murderous Use of Water Award in 2013
The Telltale Death and *Beef Killington* also tied for first place in the Central Valley Writers Workshop Competition in 2011.

Although the stories all take place in California's Central Valley, as dictated by the rules of the competition, all locations are fictitious or used fictitiously. All characters and events come directly from my slightly twisted mind and have no connection to any real person, dead or alive. No part of this publication may be reproduced, stored in or introduced into a retrieval system, or transmitted in any form, or by any means (electronic, photocopying, recording or otherwise) except for short quotes for review purposes only, without prior written permission of the publisher and copyright owner of this book. Copyright by Susan Tuttle (2008, 2009 and 2013 respectively)

A Writer Within Publication
All rights reserved
ISBN-10: 1941465145
ISBN-13: 978-1-941465-14-1

WRITER WITHIN

Dedication

This trio of stories are dedicated to Sisters in Crime (SinC), a fantastic organization who supports both writers and readers of mysteries, suspense and thrillers. And especially to the fantastic steering committee who started it,
fantastic writers all:

Sara Paretsky, Nancy Pickard, Charlotte MacLeod, Kate Mattes, Betty Francis, Dorothy Salisbury Davis and Susan Dunlap

Thanks for helping make it easier for all of us women who love
the mysterious and arcane.

Contents

Acknowledgments

No writer can produce an engaging, well-written work of fiction without the input, help and encouragement of other writers. I am blessed to have some of the best in the industry around me in SLO NightWriters and the Central Coast Chapter of Sisters in Crime (SinC). And, of course, the Friday Night Writers Group, the best critique group in the world.

To all of you, I extend a heartfelt "Thank you!" for helping me be the best I can be.

For this contest, writers needed to use an object as part of the main plot. When I remembered the antique stick phone my parents had, I found the plot of this story.

The Telltale Death

Heat smothered the Central California Valley like molten lava, making every breath an effort. They stood in Lodi Memorial Cemetery around a grave piled high with fast-wilting floral tributes. Relatives, colleagues, fans and the curious stood fidgeting on yellowed grass and brass grave markers, heads bowed as the minister read interminable Bible verses. Only a few, Howard Crowe knew, mourned with sincere grief; most rejoiced in secret. William Duling, the bombastic, egocentric literary giant, had died. Lives would change, many for the better. Especially Serena Duling's.

Tall trees ringed the area, but none grew near enough to provide shelter from the triple-digit temperature. Rivulets of sweat ran beneath Howard's chambray shirt, dark circles forming wet targets on his chest and back. Light glinted from a nearby headstone and he winced, aware of how many restless gazes shifted around the gathered circle, how many wagging tongues craved release from the silence of prayer. Did it show, he wondered, the way he quivered inside, the way his mind quailed at the sight of this grave? Did his tangled thoughts peer through the thick lenses of his spectacles?

He stood stone still, afraid any movement would draw attention to himself. Looking away might seem rude and set tongues wagging. Closing his eyes could make him appear bored, raising speculation. And looking at Serena Duling would break his heart. He had no choice but to clench both hands and jaw, stare at the urn that contained William Duling's ashes and try not to gag. The brushed and polished bronze container, shaped like the epic novels Duling wrote, glimmered like cold fire in the blazing sunlight. It cost almost as much as Crowe's monthly salary. Howard knew; he had written the check.

Well, Serena could afford large expenditures now. He must not begrudge that the first of her money had been spent on Duling's funeral bier, a receptacle as overblown as the writer had been. But Howard wished she had purchased something solely for her own pleasure, a bit of payback for all she had been denied over the years. Howard didn't expect to see Serena Duling again after today. He'd wanted to leave carrying more tangible proof of her happiness than merely his hope for it.

The minister wound down at last, wiped his dripping brow with a white handkerchief, and thanked the assemblage for their attention. People stirred, fanned themselves with hands and funeral programs, and created a background drone that somehow added to the day's heat. The minister's shadow obscured Serena's expression as he bent and murmured in her ear. She nodded, brushing fingers over wet cheeks before rising. The crowd dispersed but Howard remained in place, loath to give up a moment of Serena's presence. Then his heart began to thud. Serena skirted the hole in which the urn would rest and headed straight for him. He swallowed and forced his face to remain passive, hoping he looked at least a little saddened by her loss. *Do not meet her eyes, do not let her see*, he told himself, even as their eyes met.

"Howard," she said, her smoky voice pitched low and intimate. "How good of you to come today."

"Oh. Yes. Of course, Mrs. Duling." His voice issued forth in breathless hitches; Howard felt his face burn red. "This has been s-s-s," he shook his head, forced words through the embarrassing constriction, "very hard on all of us. It happened s-s-so quickly. Quite a sh-sh-sh," he closed his eyes, counted to three, took a breath, "blow."

"Yes," Serena said, her eyes compassionate as she waited for him to finish his painful speech. Then she bit her lip and turned her head away. "I have a favor to ask, if you're willing."

Howard's heart leapt into his throat. He swallowed it down, forcing himself not to turn and flee.

"Oh. Yes. Anything, Mrs. Duling." She held out her hands. He stared at them a full ten seconds before daring to reach out and clasp them in his. "I'll do my best."

"I – I need to get away for a while," she said. Her hands trembled and Howard tightened his fingers. "The shock, it's quite undone me. I have a distant cousin not too far from here, in Victor, I can stay with

her until I'm strong again. A week or two. Could you
—" She took a deep breath; it stuttered in her throat.
"Would you stay in the house while I'm away to take
care of Tinker Belle? And arrange William's papers,
organize things, do what needs to be done?" She
looked into his eyes and again her tone lowered, grew
intimate. "The publisher keeps asking for his last book,
and the attorney has phoned about contracts and such.
I don't think I can face coming home to it. Would you?"

Howard clamped his jaw to keep in a shout of
joy. Another week or two in her house, among her
things. It barely mattered that her dumb cat would be
there and she wouldn't, or that Duling had died in the
place. He permitted a tiny smile to curl his lips.

"Of course I will, Mrs. Duling. I'm honored you
think me worthy of s-s-s-such a task."

"My husband trusted few people in his life,
Howard, yet he found you worthy to assist him. How
could I do otherwise when you've been so kind to
me?"

Howard felt his eyes fill at her praise. He
ducked his head lest she see.

"Is there anything else you need me to do, Mrs.
Duling?" he asked when he could trust his voice again.

"Yes. Call me Serena, Howard. Please. I must go
now, Cousin Althea is waiting." Her pale lilac-blue
eyes stared into his, her auburn curls an ethereal cloud
haloing her head. Time stood still. Her sad smile
melted his heart. "I don't know how I would have
managed without you. I can't thank you enough."

And then she was gone, leaving Howard
standing alone beside William Duling's grave, the key
to her house in his hand.

* * *

The century-old red cedar home, painted pristine white, sheltered beneath tall pines and white birch trees on West Vine Street, just two blocks from the Southern Pacific rail line. Twice a day a train's haunting wail wafted through the area. Serena had painted each room a different pastel color. Large windows flooded the place with light that gleamed on ancient oak floors and warmed the comfortable upholstered furnishings. Antiques filled the home; even Duling's den had a vintage stick telephone, the only phone in the room. It sat on a small mahogany side table against the wall opposite Duling's massive cherry desk. The phone's black lacquered stem looked showroom new; the brushed brass trumpet and earpiece gleamed in the room's ambient light. Neither dust nor fingerprint marred its virginal surface.

Howard had never been in Duling's inner sanctum before, though he'd caught glimpses of it from the main hallway. Duling had dictated ideas, random thoughts and character sketches into a tape recorder, which Howard had transcribed in his own cramped office at the back of the house off the kitchen, while Duling wrote his novels in secret in his den. Howard also typed Duling's correspondence, kept Duling's books and ran Duling's errands. Howard was pretty sure the tiny space allotted him had once been a closet of some sort.

He'd spent the first day after the funeral hauling files of legal forms and contracts from the main office into his mini-space, jumping at every creak of floorboard, rustle of bush against window, scrape of tree branch across tile roof. He'd actually shrieked twice when Tinker Belle had wound around his legs, seeking attention and food. But lack of adequate space eventually defeated him, forced him to brave Duling's den and work at Duling's desk. Howard couldn't quite manage to slow his racing heart or keep his mind fully on his assigned tasks. Duling's powerful invisible presence radiated from walls and shelves which displayed the writer's trophies and certificates, his Nobel Prize Medal, framed newspaper clippings and photographs of Duling with mayors, governors and other erudite luminaries, two past Presidents and the current Pope. Howard kept expecting the man to appear in the doorway to grind him under his heel.

At noon on the third day he went into the kitchen for lunch. He made an egg salad sandwich and tea for himself, fed the cat the remains of his chicken dinner from the night before, and thumbed through Serena's rose scrapbook while he ate, hoping to calm his nerves. He'd unearthed the album from its hiding place in the living room window seat the night before. Award certificates from the Lodi Rose Society lay secreted between the leather covers, separated by photos and articles on her achievements from the Lodi News Sentinel. He looked at the slim vase of peach-colored roses that he'd found on Serena's nightstand and brought into the kitchen to keep him company. She'd won her first award for that rose bush, five years ago. Howard leafed through the scrapbook until he located the crinkled certificate.

"Look, darling," Howard had heard her say to Duling when she'd come home. He'd caught a glimpse of her through the open door of his closet, fair complexion excitement-heightened, pale eyes laughing with happiness. "I've won! Best of show, can you believe it? I wish you'd been there for the awards ceremony."

She'd handed Duling an elaborate parchment certificate stamped with the seal of the Lodi Rose Society. Duling's face had twisted into a moue of distaste.

"A floral competition may amuse those of stunted intellectual capacity, Serena, but my work is much too important to be cast aside for something so paltry. After all, it is only flowers. You stick them into the ground and they grow. Anyone can do it." He tossed the certificate, crushed from his grip, onto the counter. "I trust dinner will not be late."

Duling had returned to his office without a backward glance. Serena smoothed out the certificate and hid it away. As the years passed, Howard had left small post-it congratulations for Serena on the kitchen counter whenever he spotted a rose photo or article in the paper, or saw her bring home another award and place it between the album pages without mentioning it to Duling. The excitement had faded from her face; deep sadness filled her eyes. Dinner was never late.

Howard drained his teacup, set it with the saucer atop the empty sandwich plate, and put them in the sink to wash later. He left the scrapbook on the kitchen table, pleased that Serena wouldn't have to hide her accomplishments anymore. She could hang her awards on every wall; Duling could never again belittle her, or hurt her.

The phone rang. Howard jumped, startled by the bell's loud intrusion on the silence. He stood at the counter with his hand on the receiver through five more rings before answering it.

"Duling residence," he all but whispered. "How may I help you?"

"Howard?" Serena's sweet voice caressed his ear; he almost dropped the receiver. "Is everything all right? I can hardly hear you."

"Oh. Yes, Mrs. Duling," he said, wondering if she could hear his racketing heartbeat through the wire. "Everything is fine."

"Serena, please. I'm still here in Victor. But I've been worried about you." Her voice deepened, grew sensual. "I feel bad that I left you with so much work. Have you made much headway on the papers?"

"Oh. Yes." Howard pressed a hand to his forehead and concentrated all his energy on pronouncing one glorious word. "S-Serena." He breathed a sigh of relief. "I have just finished with the legal papers and am about to begin on the research files."

"I do hope you're not in that cramped little space William gave you?"

"I was, but it is much more efficient to work in the main office. I do hope that meets with your approval, Mrs. – uh, S-Serena."

"Of course you must use William's office. It's hard enough work, you may as well be comfortable while you're at it. I shall be very upset if you do not use his office."

"No. I mean, yes. I mean," Howard stammered. "If that is what you want, of course I will remain there."

"Good. And Tinker Belle? Does she miss me?"

"Uh." Howard glanced at the cat, sound asleep on top of the refrigerator, and told Serena what he knew she wanted to hear. "S-she is inconsolable."

Serena sighed; the sound's sadness wavered down Howard's spine. They talked a few minutes more about Serena's rose garden and trivial household matters.

"Thank you, Howard," Serena purred at last. "I feel much better knowing I need no longer worry about the house. Or you. You are a treasure, you know. It's easy to see why William relied on you for everything. Goodbye."

Howard floated into Duling's office, Serena's praise ringing in his ears. A treasure! Serena had called him a treasure. The task ahead of him no longer looked quite so daunting, occupying the house not quite as nerve-wracking. He worked steadily for an hour, first organizing the three file drawers of short stories. Then he lifted up the thick manuscript Duling had finished just days before his massive coronary. Howard laid his hand on the stack of nine hundred eight pages, work no other eyes than Duling's had yet seen, and read the title. *Death Duties.* He sighed, thinking of the huge advance Duling's publisher had bestowed, sight unseen. Howard had given up dreams of huge advances—of any advances—for his own writing. Duling's prolific output and time-consuming demands had left Howard no room for his own creativity.

Serena's high praise gave him courage. He glanced around the room, half expecting Duling's ghost to appear, then began turning pages, skimming the printed words to glean the story-line. He had to force himself not to become immersed in the compelling prose; though a monstrous human being, Duling had written as though angels guided his pen. The murderer struck a third of the way into the novel. Howard read the scene a dozen times before he re-stacked the pages, loath now to even touch the manuscript.

A variation. The bastard had used Serena's idea with a few minor changes. Howard winced as he remembered the devastation Duling had wrought that day. Howard had just left the kitchen after refilling his coffee mug. Serena and Duling sat at the kitchen table, sharing a mid-morning snack. Duling's words, obviously a continuation of a conversation curtailed by Howard's entry into the room, had stopped Howard's feet in the back hallway.

"It's got to be untraceable, damn it," Duling had said with his usual surliness. "Whole plot hinges on that."

"I have an idea, darling," Serena said, her tone tentative, almost frightened.

"You? Do tell."

The derision in Duling's voice had made Howard's hands spasm on the mug; drops of coffee splotched onto the brown carpet. He'd held his breath, shrank into the shadows against the corridor wall, and peered into the kitchen. Serena's mouth had tightened. She turned her head and looked at where Howard stood with no sign of recognition in her eyes.

"I read somewhere," she said, turning back to look at Duling, "that potassium chloride, in a large enough dose, will trigger a heart attack in a healthy person. A massive one."

"Serena," Duling had said in his talking-to-a-backward-child tone, "I need something clever."

"But this is clever, darling. No one would suspect poison if someone dies of a heart attack. And the article said—"

"Some ridiculous article?" Duling waved a dismissing hand in her face. "Really, Serena. My readers are discerning and intelligent. I need something they don't already know."

Serena had stared at Duling, then looked into her coffee cup.

"I didn't know it," she'd murmured. Duling rose.

"My point, exactly," he'd said, and walked out of the kitchen toward his den.

Serena had stood and stared after her husband, her chin trembling, her hands clenched at her sides.

"It would work," she'd murmured, her gaze on his retreating back, "especially if the person were overweight and careless about his health. And sedentary. Like you."

She'd caught her breath then let it out with a little shake of her head. Again she looked over at where Howard had stood rooted in the gloomy back hall, the expression in her eyes miles away and infinitely sad. Howard wasn't sure she saw him even though her gaze had seemed fixed on his face.

"If only..." she said.

Then she'd shuddered, rubbed her hands along her arms as if chilled, and left the room.

The phone rang as Howard shoved the manuscript aside. He looked across at where the stick phone stood on the side table, wondering if he should answer it. Five rings; no answering machine clicked on and Howard remembered that Duling had hated them, had refused to install one. *Could Serena be calling again?* he wondered. *This soon?* Howard doubted it. Eight rings; he probably should answer it, perhaps it was Duling's agent or publisher. He rose and crossed to the side table, raised the slim stick phone up to his lips, then lifted the earpiece and pressed it against his ear.

"Duling residence," he said. "How may I help you?"

Silence answered him. He frowned.

"Hello? Who is this?"

A faint burst of static echoed in his ear and plucked at his strained nerves. He listened for a few seconds but could detect no voice, no words. He clicked the earpiece cradle a few times, heard nothing more, then hung up the earpiece.

He went back to the desk, unaccountably disturbed, trying to convince himself that it was probably kids fooling around. Or maybe there was trouble on the line. He sat down and the phone rang again. He gave it twelve rings this time before he once again crossed to the phone.

"Who is this?" he asked into the mouthpiece.

Again, silence. Then, very faint, very far away, a tapping at his ears; th-thum, th-thum, th-thum. A pause, then; th-thum, th-thum, th-thum.

Howard dropped the earpiece onto the cradle. The phone rang again before he could set the stick part down. He snatched at the earpiece.

"What?" he shouted.

Th-thum, louder this time, nearer. Th-thum!

Howard's breath strangled in his throat.

"What is this?" he choked. "What's happening?"

The stick slipped from his numb fingers onto the table. He stood a moment, gasping, then reached out and slammed the earpiece down onto the cradle. He couldn't move, couldn't think.

The phone rang again.

Howard jerked and ran to the windows. He yanked the curtains closed, then peered out a tiny crack, scanning the bushes, the sidewalks, the neighbor's house. The only moving thing in sight was a silver SUV that went past the house without a pause. The phone kept ringing.

Howard backed into a corner and stood with his hands over his ears until the ringing finally stopped. He stood watching the phone for ten minutes, but it remained silent. He was still trembling when he went back to the desk.

"It's just kids, that's all," he muttered with a shaky laugh. "It's this house, his things, the memories. You're well now; get a grip. Don't do this to yourself."

Two hours later, the phone rang again. Howard had himself under control this time. He answered it on the third ring.

Th-thum! The insistent heartbeat drove at him.

He shuddered despite his resolve and closed his eyes, his own heart tattooing in his chest. He counted to five, opened his eyes and hung up, then lifted the earpiece and laid it on the table beside the phone.

"Sorry, kids, that's the end of that," he said.

It rang again. Howard clicked the cradle up and down. The phone kept ringing.

"But it's off the hook. It can't be ringing!" Howard whispered.

The ringing stopped and again the heart sound echoed into the room. Howard's hand reached out of its own volition and raised the earpiece. Two sounds, now, the persistent heartbeat entwined with faint, gasping breaths. Th-thum, *rasp*.

His fingers opened. The earpiece bounced onto the table. Howard backed into the corner, his breath shuddering in his throat. The phone fell silent. Twenty minutes later it rang yet again. Howard moaned and slid down the wall, hands over his ears.

Ghastly sounds spewed from the phone and reverberated around the room. They hammered at Howard, frozen in the corner. On and on; silence, then ringing, then the horrific sounds of death. A stuttering heartbeat and strangled breathing. And a voice, grating, barely audible, saying—what? His name? His name! No matter where he went, which room he was in, indoors or out, the sounds followed him, invaded him, pulsed in time to his own heartbeat: *th-thum, rasp, Howard!*

"Stop! Stop!" Howard screamed, running from the property. "I confess! I did it, I killed you! Leave me alone, leave me alone!"

The police had never seen anything like the madman who raced through their doors as though the hounds of hell were after him, shouting about a ringing phone, death rattles and confessing to murder.

* * *

Serena hurried home when the police called to tell her of Crowe's confession and requested an interview. They met her at the front door. Dark, burly Detective Sanchez sat in the living room on the chintz-covered couch. His partner, greyhound-lean Lisa Calloway, stood in the archway. Serena sat opposite Sanchez on an upholstered armchair and toyed with her diamond wedding band as she answered his long list of questions.

"No, I haven't read William's latest manuscript. He never let anyone read his works in progress. Like everyone else, I have to wait until the books are published." She gave a slight shrug. "I don't even know the title."

"Crowe said he got the idea to kill your husband from the manuscript," Sanchez said. "How could that be if he hadn't read it?"

"I don't know." Serena looked at Sanchez and shook her head. "He did transcribe William's notes, though."

"His notes?"

"Yes. Details to be worked into the novel, character sketches, ideas for scenes, things like that. William used a tape recorder, Howard typed them up, and William worked off the printed copies."

"Then that's it." Sanchez looked at Calloway and they nodded. "Duling must have dictated a note on the murder and Howard used it himself."

"But I don't understand," Serena said, her voice soft and hesitant. "You're saying that Howard Crowe murdered my husband? Why would he do such a thing?"

"Did you know him well, Mrs. Duling?" Sanchez asked.

"Not really." She shook her head. "He worked with William. I knew him to say hello to, is about all. I never spent any time with him. And William never left us alone together."

"Why is that, Mrs. Duling?" Calloway asked.

"Howard had had a breakdown of sorts a few years ago, William told me he'd been hospitalized for it. Howard seemed to me like a nice young man, if terribly timid, and he was a competent enough assistant." She paused and frowned. "But William always kept him well occupied and away from me. I don't think William entirely trusted Howard for all that he felt sorry for him."

"That agrees with what Crowe told us, Mrs. Duling," Sanchez said, "that you had no hand in what he did, no knowledge of it. He seemed to think you were unhappy in your marriage, that your husband was mistreating you. Said he wanted to free you from his tyranny."

"Tyranny? William and I had arguments, of course, what married couple doesn't?" She raised her hands in a supplicating gesture. "But we were happy, very much in love. I don't know what I shall do without him." She blinked her eyes clear of tears. "But the doctors said he died of a heart attack. How could that be murder?"

"He was poisoned," Sanchez said. "Crowe told us that after you left for the Rose Society meeting, he spiked your husband's tea water with potassium chloride, then left to do errands. When your husband made and drank his mid-morning tea, he ingested a massive dose of the poison. It triggered a fatal heart attack. Potassium chloride's almost undetectable in the body unless we specifically test for it." Sanchez shrugged. "Since your husband was overweight and sedentary, it appeared to be a cut-and-dried heart attack. We didn't know to look further."

Serena shook her head. "But Mr. Crowe had gotten away with it. What made him confess?"

Detective Calloway shifted in the archway and made a derisive noise deep in her throat.

"He's crazy," she said.

"Claimed Duling called him from the grave," Sanchez added, "and hounded him through the telephone in your den. Kept raving about heartbeats and dying breaths."

"The phone in the den?" Serena looked at Detective Calloway, then back at Sanchez. "That's impossible. Are you sure?" Sanchez nodded and Serena rose. "Come with me, please."

She led the detectives to the den where a fire burned in the grate. She picked up the stick phone, pulled up the cord and rolled the long, loose wire around her hand.

"My husband was a bit eccentric," she told the detectives. "He hated to be disturbed when writing. There is no working phone in this room. This is an antique, a valuable one. The wire cannot be connected to today's technology without destroying that value."

"Like we said," Sanchez scratched his half-bald head, "the guy's nutso. A real lunatic. I'm just glad he's off the streets. You take care, now." He patted her shoulder. "We'll let ourselves out."

Serena watched through the den window as the detectives climbed into their car and drove off. Then she laughed and stretched her arms above her head.

"Freedom," she said. "And money. Thank you, Howard Crowe, for being so easy. I couldn't have done it without you."

She turned the stick phone over, pried off the base and removed the mini tape recorder. She clicked it on. *Th-thum!* echoed in the room. She removed the tape and threw it in the fireplace. Then she took a ball peen hammer from a desk drawer, pulled a remote device off the bottom of the small table and smashed it to pieces. They followed the tape into the fire.

"And I appreciate your help, too," she said to the vintage phone as she polished away Howard Crowe's fingerprints with a soft cloth, restoring the instrument's mellow glow.

She set the phone back on the table, the disconnected cord rolled into a neat bundle beside it. Smiling, she walked to the concealed wet bar on the other side of the room and poured herself a glass of Appellation Zinfandel. She paused, then ran her fingers over the albums lining one shelf, another of her husband's affectations, large old-fashioned vinyl discs dinosaured by digital technology. She pulled one out and set it on the phonograph's spindle, then put the needle on the edge of the spinning disc. The haunting strains of "That Old Black Magic" wound into the air. Serena, humming, swayed to the music as the words unrolled in her head. She laughed at the thought of icy fingers running up Howard's spine. Then she sat behind the desk and pulled out William Duling's bank ledger.

"Now, let's see just how well off you've left me, darling." she said to his picture. Her grin widened.

And the antique phone rang.

For this story, setting had to take pride of place. I let my twisted mind contemplate the Central Valley, and this idea sprang forth.

Beef Killington

Everything that composes, decomposes; what a delicious thought.

Quinn Ackey set a dirty pan in the sink, glanced out the kitchen window and smiled at her compost pile. She loved this window; it was the only one in the house that didn't look out on fields of filthy cattle, though if the wind was right it did let in the raunchy, nauseating reek of beef on the hoof. She allowed herself a few seconds to look further, to bask in the sight of the kitchen garden, lush herbs backed by sprays of lavender and flanked by ripening vegetables. This part was her domain. Not the rest of it, though; the unruly carpet of wild, sun-scorched grass, the alien-looking, spiked agave, the dangerous, ugly prickly pear, that was her husband's idea of a Western garden. If she craned her neck to the left could she see out-of-control geraniums twining up the side of the garage.

She shuddered. Geraniums should grow close to the ground, their flowers compact knobs of red. But not here; oh, no, in California's Central Valley they became unruly monsters that towered overhead and lost all resemblance to the soothing, disciplined flowers she grew up with. Here, in this dusty, smelly, smog-layered place, where stifling heat scoured clouds from the unrelenting blue sky and wicked every drop of moisture from her body, the omnipresent bellow of cattle filled her head day and night. She couldn't think or read, couldn't write, couldn't carry on a conversation without wanting to scream. Thank God the garage and a grove of rancid-smelling eucalyptus trees screened the barn and silos from view; even at a quarter mile away they were a blot on the flat landscape. But it was all right now; her five years were up and she couldn't wait to leave. If only she could get the sauce right.

The stove timer buzzed. Quinn turned from the window and snapped off the oven.

"Can I help?"

Quinn looked up and smiled at petite, blonde Victoria Dell, her closest friend, another hostage by marriage withering on Fresno's cattle vine.

"Sure, put the potatoes in that bowl, will you?"

They worked in silence for a few moments, then Victoria looked at her.

"Rowell's not back yet?" she asked in a quiet tone. Quinn stiffened.

"No." Quinn glanced at Victoria. "And I'm not sure he's coming back."

"What?"

"I've suspected for a while there was someone else, he's been so distant." Quinn pressed her lips together and shut her eyes. "A couple of weeks ago he packed a bag and walked out."

"And he hasn't called you?"

"No. I don't even know where he went. After all I've done for him, what I've given up..." She forced herself to shrug and gave Victoria a wry smile. "That's mid-life crisis, for you."

"I'm so sorry, Quinn."

"It's okay. Doesn't matter." She ran her hands over her face and took a deep breath. "How about using that bowl for the zucchini?"

"Sure. Gosh, it smells like heaven in here," Victoria said as she ladled small, translucent white balls from the pan. "What did you do to this? It's really zucchini?"

"Would I kid you?"

"I swear, you're a kitchen genius. I can't even boil water without burning it!"

Quinn laughed. She hadn't been sure, when she decided to use the melon scoop on the zucchini, if the vegetable wouldn't simply fall apart. But she'd been careful not to overcook it, and so far it was holding together. She opened the oven and drew out the roast, releasing a burst of impudent spice into the air.

"Oh, my God, what is that?" Victoria stopped, vegetable bowls in hand, and closed her eyes as she inhaled.

"My latest tri-tip contest experiment." Quinn transferred the sauce-coated roast to a cutting board and sliced thick wedges which she arranged on a platter. She spooned up the remaining sauce from the roasting pan and spread it over the sliced meat, then picked up the dish and grinned at Victoria. "Thanks for being my guinea pigs—again."

"Like it's such a hardship," Victoria said, leading the way into the dining room where her husband and their mutual friends, the Gardiners, sat waiting to eat. "I'm just glad you don't advertise for guinea pigs or the whole Valley would line up at your door. And I'd go hungry."

"Oh, you," Quinn murmured as they set the food on the table to a chorus of oohs and aahs.

Danny Gardiner barely waited for his wife, Grace, to finish the blessing before digging in. A look of rapture crossed his face. Victoria's husband, Wayne, actually groaned with his first taste of the meat. Quinn took a couple tentative bites of the roast, but she couldn't tell if it tasted right or not. She'd been experimenting for so long now she was no longer able to discern if the sauce did what it needed to do. She watched the others eat for a few moments, then raised her brows.

"Well?" she asked.

"I swear, woman, this is the best tri-tip sauce I ever tasted, even better than my Daddy's, and that's saying a lot," Danny said. "Let's bottle it. We'll make a fortune!"

Quinn's heart began to beat faster.

"I agree," Wayne said. "Incredible. Never had anything like it."

Quinn smiled and her fingers tightened on her fork. Had she done it, finally?

"But why did you put it on pork?" Grace asked. "I thought you had to use beef tri-tip for the contest."

Quinn's heart dropped. She frowned down at her plate, then forced herself to smile at her guests.

"Are you sure it's pork?" She gave them all a mock-innocent look. "The right sauce can disguise anything, you know."

They all laughed, but Quinn knew she'd failed again. And she couldn't fail, too much rode on winning this contest; her freedom, her whole future. Time was running out. She had only three more weeks to find the correct combination of tastes.

She discovered the right recipe a week later on her thirteenth try, the day Rowell's foreman brought the police to the house.

"Diego?" she asked when she opened the door, her gaze sliding past him to the uniformed patrolman standing nearby. "Is something wrong?"

"Rowell here?"

Diego's laconic cigarette-rasp grated down her spine. Quinn's hand tightened on the door frame.

"No. I haven't seen him for almost three weeks. Why?"

"He ain't been to the barn," Diego said before the tall, thin officer stepped up and moved him aside. The cop had canny green eyes, roan-colored hair too bushy for his narrow face, and bandy legs. Quinn thought he'd look more comfortable in rodeo denim than clad in law-enforcement khaki. His name badge read, P. Estrada.

"Mr. Morales here's reported Mr. Ackey missing, ma'am," Estrada drawled in a voice like warm cream. "Wonderin' why you haven't, being the wife and all."

"I didn't know he was missing," Quinn said.

"Seems he is. You mind if we look around a bit, check over the grounds?"

"Not at all." She opened the door to let Officer Estrada into the house. "Look wherever you need to. I'll be in the kitchen."

"Lotta his clothes gone from the bedroom," Estrada said after he'd moseyed through the house and sauntered into the kitchen.

"Yes," Quinn said.

Estrada refused the coffee she offered and folded his lanky frame onto a stool at the island counter. Quinn stirred the pot on the stove, then opened the oven to ladle more sauce over her roast. She picked up her cup and looked at Estrada over the rim.

"As embarrassing as it is to admit," she said, looking back down at the coffee, "Rowell left me about three weeks ago. We'd had words." She paused and bit her lip. "I think he's been seeing someone else. He packed a bag and stormed out." She sighed and looked up at Estrada.

"He hasn't contacted you at all?"

"No. I guess I really didn't expect to hear from him. His lawyer, maybe, but not Rowell." She frowned. "Still, it's not like him to neglect the ranch. I assumed he was at the barn every day, like usual. The cattle are his life." Movement outside the window caught her attention; five uniformed men, two leading black labs, quartered her garden. Alarm flushed through her. "What's going on out there?"

"We're just looking," Estrada said, his eyes flat and unreadable when she turned to look at him. "In case Mr. Ackey's still around here somewhere."

"But, dogs?"

"No stone unturned, you know?" Estrada said, joining her at the window. "You mind?"

"No. Why would I?" Quinn said, her heart thudding.

She stared out the window as the canines circled the yard to approach the compost pile and Estrada gauged her reaction. Quinn licked her lips and tried not to hold her breath. The Labs inched across the mucky dirt, noses vacuuming every inch, bodies quivering, stopping here and there. Time elongated. Quinn desperately wanted more coffee, but her hands felt too shaky to lift the pot. The dogs finally shook themselves, snorted and moved off to another part of the garden, their sweating handlers plodding after them.

"Interesting to watch them work," Quinn said as she filled her cup with steady hands. Estrada sat down again.

Twenty minutes later Quinn took the small roast from the oven and held it out to Officer Estrada.

"It's my entry for the tri-tip contest. Can I tempt you?"

"I'm not supposed to accept anything, ma'am. But doggone it, that sure smells wonderful. You won't tell anyone, will you?"

He was halfway through a slice when two of his men knocked on the back door to report that nothing had been found by either officers or the search dogs.

"Good, that's good," Estrada said. "Uh, could they try this, too, Mrs. Ackey? You won't believe it," he told the men when Quinn nodded and they filed into the kitchen, "it's the best damn tri-tip I've ever had—begging pardon, ma'am."

The men raved about the beef roast nestled in its coat of savory sauce. Quinn and Estrada took their coffee mugs onto the back porch while the men finished eating.

"I've been working for weeks on the sauce," Quinn told Estrada. "I hope it's good enough."

"Ain't just the sauce, it's the whole package. I know my tri-tip and yours is superb. Fantastic." He took a sip of coffee; Quinn repressed a shout of joy. "What are you going to do with it now? It's a gourmet contest this year, right? Can't serve it like regular tri-tip, can you?"

"I have an idea," Quinn said, giving him a coy look, her heart doing a victory dance in her chest, "but it's a deep, dark secret. Wouldn't want anyone to steal my thunder, you know?"

"Sure do." Estrada chuckled. "My Pa enters that damn contest every year, never lets anyone taste his beforehand. You'd think national security was at risk." He nodded at her yard. "Great garden you got there. What's the secret?"

"The compost." Quinn smiled at the unsightly mound. "Ground eggshells, coffee grounds, kitchen scraps. And bone meal. Works every time."

Quinn saw the men out and, with their praise still ringing in her ears, went into the kitchen to finalize her entry for the Central Valley Gourmet Tri-Tip Contest.

* * *

Quinn watched the judges' faces as they tasted the entries, but she learned nothing. They took great care to hide their reactions behind exaggerated winks, pokes, lip smacks and laughter. Her clenched hands shook as the interminable day inched on. She refused to let her mind play "what if?" games.

The Tri-Tip Festival sprawled as usual on Rowell's flat, dry north acreage. Sweat rivered down her face, back and sides, plastering her silk blouse to her body. Smog smudged the pale blue sky and hazed over a sun that pulsated with heat. The reek of manure layered the air. Dust wormed into her nose; she'd sneezed a dozen or more times already. The only shade came from awnings erected over the food stalls. Since the gates had opened at ten a.m. throngs of people had converged on the stands to sample beef tri-tip in all its many guises. Barrels filled with discarded paper plates stood at the corner of each booth. Quinn didn't know how anyone could eat so much heavy, rich food in this suffocating heat.

But now it was time to hand out awards. The Master of Ceremonies stood on a raised dais, holding a microphone. He yelled for quiet. It took a few minutes, but gradually the only sounds left were small babies fussing and the ubiquitous bawling of cattle.

"The judges have made their decision!" said Derek Guarnera, chairman of this year's contest and inspiration behind the gourmet theme. "It was sure tough having to taste all these wonderful entries, but our panel somehow managed." The crowd laughed and Guarnera motioned for silence. "It is my pleasure to award the third place ribbon and five hundred dollars to," he paused and the suspense built, suspense

Quinn could have done without, "Shirley Frazier, for her Tri-Tip Barbecue Quiche!"

The crowed cheered and chubby, gray-haired Shirley bobbed up to receive her ribbon and check, her face flaming red with delight and embarrassment.

"Now, second place, and a thousand dollars, goes to, drum roll, please," he said to the judges, who obliged by beating on the table with their fingers, "Paul Palumbo, for his entry, Oriental Tri-Tip Surprise with Wild Rice!"

Again, the crowd went wild as Paul, a locally-famous chef, strode to the podium in apron and toque, his expression a mixture of pleasure and disappointment. This time it took Guarnera a few minutes to calm the audience. Quinn's heartbeat accelerated to lightning speed. She wiped her hands on her damp linen slacks. *Please*, she thought; *please*.

"And our top prize, ten thousand dollars and a year in France at the Cordon Bleu, goes to—and this was, according to the judges, the most outstanding entry, far eclipsing any of the others." Guarnera paused to look around the crowd as though searching for someone. When he met Quinn's eyes, he smiled. "It goes to Quinn Ackey for her Tri-Tip Wellington!"

"Yes!" Quinn shouted.

She raced up to collect her blue ribbon and prize certificates, the crowd's cheers almost deafening. Guarnera put a sweaty arm around her. From the corner of her eye she saw the judges portion out the last of her Wellington onto their plates.

"Tell me, Quinn," Guarnera said, shoving the microphone in her face, "what made you think of taking barbecue tri-tip and wrapping it in pate and pastry like a Wellington? What inspired you?"

"It was my husband's idea," she told Guarnera.

And she thought about the fight she'd had with Rowell. She'd insisted he honor his promise that they would return to New York City after five years on the cattle ranch. He'd accomplished his goal of breeding cattle whose meat was more tender, richer and tastier the older the cattle got. But no. He'd already found another cause, a new cross-breed, that would entail a move to a Brazilian jungle where their nearest neighbor would be five miles away. Total isolation for Quinn. She'd told him she would divorce him, take his money and go back home by herself. "Over my dead body!" he'd roared.

Victoria ran up and hugged her.

"You did it! I'm so happy for you! My God, France! And the Cordon Bleu!"

Quinn pulled a linen handkerchief from her pocket and wiped dusty sweat from her face. She looked down at her certificates, pressed them to her chest and looked over at the judges eating up the last of her prize-winning entry. She smiled at Victoria.

"France." Quinn sighed aloud; no more cattle, no more dust and sweat, no more manure. "It's a dream come true. But I'll miss you terribly."

"And me you." Victoria hugged her again. "It's too bad Rowell isn't here for this."

"Oh, but he is." Quinn reached over, snagged the last morsel of Wellington from the serving platter and popped it into Victoria's mouth. "He is."

The theme for the contest for this year was "water rights and wrongs." The minute I heard that, the entire plot for this story burst in my head.

Hydro-Synth

"How many bodies?"

Detective Juan Rodriguez stood in the sand between Fresno and Madera, stared down at the pit and tried to guess. It wasn't very deep, which was why the elements had been able to bare a leathery forearm and hand to curious eyes. Desert winds wailed around him, peppering him with grit, and he hunched his shoulders. Joe Lapin, the medical examiner, looked up, shielding his eyes with a blue gloved hand.

"Looks like nine to me," he said. He shook his head. "No IDs. Ain't got a clue when they died. Or how. When I get them to the lab I'll figure it out."

"How long to get like that out here?" Rodriguez looked around at the blowing sand, the stunted cactus. At fifty-four, he was old enough to remember his granddad's dairy ranch. Fenced fields, green grass, cows and cattle as far as the eye could see. Of course, that was before the end of the ozone layer. Before the water dried up. Before California's San Joaquin Valley became the new Dust Bowl.

"Mummified?" Lapin's voice recalled him to the present. "Depends, a few weeks in ideal conditions. Lots longer if they're buried like this. These bodies look decades old, but," he held up an arm on which a laser watch glittered in the sunlight, "this sure isn't. Something's not right, here."

"Might be impossible to identify them." Rodriguez looked again at the surrounding desert and shuddered. "Sometimes I hate this job."

He turned and trudged through the sand to Highway 99 where his cruiser waited, a scant hundred feet from the burial site. Which is why the upthrust hand had been noticed. Vehicles, no matter how well sealed, were no match for the baking heat, the wind and the sand. Breakdowns were common, and anything that disturbed the flatness of the landscape drew attention. Had whoever it was dug the hole deeper, he wouldn't be out here now, and he wouldn't have nine murder cases to deal with. Sometime life just sucked.

How much it sucked he discovered when he ran the prints that Lapin, using a newly-developed colloidal technique, had managed to raise on three of the dried-out corpses. Teeth clenched, he punched in the morgue's number.

"The fuck you doing to me?" he growled when Lapin answered. "Adrienne got her hands on a new Hydro-synth veggie, and it's waiting for me at home. Why am I here with you and not there?"

"You tell me." Laskin's curt tone betrayed the jealousy Rodriguez knew he felt because Rodriguez could afford Hydro-synth veggies and he couldn't. Not that Rodriguez's salary was that big. His wife headed a marketing firm that had Hydro-synth as its main client. "The prints," Rodriguez said, feeling stomach acid churn at the thought of the dinner he would miss. "What about them? Thought you'd be happy I got them so fast."

"So did I, 'til I ran them. I thought you said it took weeks, plural, to mummify a body."

"That's right. Three, minimum, but most likely four or five. In ideal conditions. But we don't have ideal conditions out there, starting with they were buried. Why?"

"Cause I'm looking at a print match—

"That was quick," Laskin said. Rodriguez ignored him.

"—to an Andrew Cho, reported missing last week. According to his wife, he left for work on Tuesday morning and never came home."

"But that's only, uh, nine days. I don't think…"

"What?" Rodriguez was well used to Lapin's pauses. They usually presaged an insight of some magnitude.

"I found no sign of decomp. Not in any of the organs. Which is not possible. Even in ideal conditions, the organs would at least begin to decay before drying out. And you can't mummify someone in nine days. We've got a real puzzler, here."

"Yeah, an enigma inside a mystery wrapped in a riddle," Rodriguez muttered. He'd read that somewhere and for the first time he understood what it meant. "And I have to solve it."

* * *

Cho's wife, Liu Yung, sat in dry-eyed stoic silence after hearing that her husband's body had been discovered. She spoke only when asked a direct question, and told him nothing new in her soft Taiwanese-accented English that Rodriguez had to lean forward to hear. Frustrated, he left her house, went back to the cruiser and called up the route to the Hydro-synth plant. Then he leaned back and let the autopilot take over.

He could still taste last night's eggplant, one of the delightful benefits of Hydro-synth grown vegetables. Most ground-grown foods had an underlying foul taste, caused by the waste water used for irrigation. Fresh water was in too short a supply to use to water plants. But the synthetic "water" developed by the Hydro-synth chemists and engineers left their vegetables bursting with flavor that lasted for hours, and with double the vitamins and minerals of natural vegetables. Too bad only the very rich could afford them, but Hydro-synth's synthetic water process, according to the literature, had cost billions to develop and millions each year to maintain. Rodriguez thanked his lucky stars that his wife was on the short list for beta test-tasting. They had Hydro-synth veggies at least twice a week.

Andrew Cho, it turned out, had worked in the development lab, part of the team charged with improving the Hydro-synth process. They'd made great strides. Rodriguez still remembered the cardboard taste of vegetables grown by the brand-new Hyrdo-synth process thirty years ago. Then, about seventeen years ago, a breakthrough led to today's fine vegetable specimens. Cho's supervisor, Grace Barrigan, a tall, stately woman with iron-gray hair and long blood-red nails, shook her head and clasped her hands when apprised of Cho's death. But no sorrow showed in her eyes.

"I knew it had to be bad." She looked over at the file cabinet in the corner. "Poor Andrew. He never missed work. Not once in the last ten years."

"What was he working on?" Rodriguez asked, intrigued that she would not look at him directly.

"Oh," Barrigan waved her hand in dismissal, her gaze now fastened on the office door, "the usual. Checking Al Foster's work, mainly. I can't give you specifics. Patent law, you know."

"Was his work critical to whatever's in development?" He watched her closely, noting the way her eyes blinked and her body stiffened. *Something's up here*, he thought.

"Critical? No, of course not." She gave an unconvincing little laugh. "The First Tier Team does all the real work. Cho's department was mainly housekeeping. If you know what I mean."

Rodriguez didn't, but he didn't ask for clarification. He requested instead to see Cho's workspace. Barrigan popped up from behind her desk with an insincere smile and escorted him to Lab #5.

Cho's desk and adjacent work counter were neat and spotless. Empty vials and clean instruments lined the wall shelves. A microscope sat in the center of the workspace. A daily calendar sat on the desktop. The pages of past dates were missing. The top page showed last Wednesday, the day after Cho vanished. The wastebasket held only a pristine liner. The desk drawers were empty of everything except a blank pad of paper, and some pens, paperclips and rubber bands. Rodriguez looked a question at Barrigan, who stood leaning on the file cabinet.

"Andrew was compulsively neat," she said, her tone defying him to challenge her.

"So I see." Rodriguez moved toward the file cabinet. Barrigan didn't move. "May I?" He gestured to the cabinet.

"Absolutely not. Not without a warrant. Our process is proprietary, Detective, and what Andrew was working on had nothing to do with what happened to him. I cannot allow you to paw through these files. It's a security issue, you understand."

Rodriguez nodded, convinced now that something was going on at Hydro-synth. Every trace of what Cho had been working on had been expunged, even before they supposedly knew about his death. There was a connection there, he was sure of it. He headed back to the office and applied for a warrant to unlock the cabinet in Cho's impossibly clean office.

It was denied. The Lieutenant ordered Rodriguez to label the case a "stranger murder" with no leads, close it and shelve it with the cold cases. True, there were no leads on any of the other bodies, except two: one, a man of fifty or so, whose prints hit in a military database. He'd been a drifter since demobilization after the Turkmenistan War of 2036, had no friends, no family. The other was a woman who had been arrested twenty years ago for solicitation and had flown under the radar ever since. None of the others were in any of the databases he searched.

It was, on the face of it, an impossible case to solve, given that six of the bodies could not even be identified. But the woman had only been dead an estimated two months, which was cutting it close for mummification as far as Rodriguez was concerned. And there was Cho, who hadn't been dead long enough to mummify under any known conditions. And there was Hydro-synth's stonewalling.

Something was very wrong at Hydro-synth. Rodriguez sat at his desk at main headquarters in City Hall and gazed out at the ruins of St. John's Cathedral, while he let the case sift through his mind. By now that incriminating file cabinet in Cho's lab on West Shaw Avenue was probably buried elsewhere in another location. Besides, he'd probably not get past security again, not with the pressure Hydro-synth had put on the Brass upstairs to bury Cho's case. Hydro-synth provided most of the jobs since the economy collapsed with the absence of water, and Fresno was already close to a ghost town. The place would shut down completely if it lost its biggest—and close to only—employer.

But Rodriguez could not let go of the puzzle. When it came to his cases he was, according to his wife, like a ravenous bulldog clamped on a man's leg. The man's leg he needed arrived in the form of a letter mailed the day before Andrew Cho died. It had been sent to the wrong station address and forwarded on three times before reaching Rodriguez's desk.

You will not believe if I tell you, the note inside read. *You must see the evil for yourself. Hydro-synth must be stopped. The proof is in the Forestiere Gardens.*

Rodriguez hadn't thought of the Gardens in years, that hand-carved subterranean world out on West Shaw Avenue that used to draw tourists by the bus-full. But it, too, had closed, dried up as had everything else in the valley. It had supposedly been filled in and the Hydro-synth labs built atop it.

But what if it hadn't been? he thought. *What if the real work of Hydro-synth went on underground?* He looked at the note signed by Andrew Cho, then called his cousin, an FBI agent in Washington. They talked a long time, then Rodriguez faxed all his records. He agreed to wait until Virgilio and his team could arrive, but he knew he wouldn't. If what he suspected was right, there wasn't a minute to waste. He checked his cell, gathered up what he would need, then left his office.

The heat hadn't abated much, even though it was past midnight. He parked six blocks away from the Hydro-synth complex and walked in the shadows the rest of the way. By the time he arrived at the rear loading docks, he was drenched in sweat.

It took only a matter of minutes to break the code on the lock and slip into the rear warehouse. He put on the night vision goggles and listened for movement as he searched for a way into the caverns below. If he was wrong, he'd feel like a fool when Virgilio arrived. If he got caught, at best he'd lose his job. At worst, they'd kill him like they had Andrew Cho.

Boxes filled the warehouse in orderly rows, most packed with luscious looking tomatoes, peppers, radishes, cucumbers, beets. He hadn't realized how extensive their greenhouses were. They had to be making a fortune with what they charged: $5.00 for one tomato; $12.00 for each cucumber. Not until he turned the corner of the last row of boxes did he find a well-hidden, narrow doorway.

Steps led down into a dimly lit hallway about twelve feet below the surface. Rodriguez stowed the goggles in his backpack and texted the info to Virgilio, who promptly responded: *Get out of there. Wait for us.* Rodriguez considered it for all of two seconds as he listened to the drone of machinery. Then he moved down the hall, checking each doorway he passed. Most opened onto tiny offices filled with a confusing array of apparatuses. One looked like a kitchenette break room. One held linens of all sorts. The last room, three times the size of the others, held the machines that hummed and clicked with relentless regularity. Just beyond, double doors awaited his hands.

He paused and took a deep breath. He'd been lucky so far, the place mostly deserted at this late hour. But he had a feeling it wouldn't last. Whatever waited on the other side of those doors, human or not, could change his life forever. He took a moment to text his love to his wife. Just in case.

He inched open the left hand door, his Magnum ready in his right hand, and sidled into an enormous cavern of a room. There was just enough light to see. He caught movement at the far end, but was too far away to tell what, or who, it was. Spread before him were rows of four-tiered bunks that marched in military precision down the length of the room. An odd sucking sound, barely audible, reverberated in the still air. Goose bumps raised on his arms, only partly caused by the cool temperature.

He inched up to the closest bunk and almost gasped aloud. A woman lay there, motionless, eyes half closed, her shrunken body barely covered by a hospital style gown. Only by concentrating could Rodriguez tell she still breathed. Tubes snaked from her chest, arms and legs into machines that stood at both head- and footboard. Moisture dripped into the catch basins on the machines. Other still forms lay in the two tiers above her.

Rodriguez felt as though he walked through a nightmare as he slinked from bunk to bunk, all occupied by human forms, all with tubes draining their moisture. He estimated 500 people lay comatose in this room, and he prayed there was not another. A noise caught his attention and he slid beneath a bunk to escape detection as two Hydro-synth chemists walked back toward the double doors.

"We're getting more out of them, faster, and with less evaporation. Cho's vacuum adjustments are brilliant," the taller one, male from the timber of voice, said. "Too bad they had to eliminate him."

"Yes, it is." That voice sounded familiar. Barrigan? "We'll have to get manufacturing turning out this new part right away. We've got more orders than we can grow, and if management reduces prices it'll only increase. Good thing there's no shortage of water vessels. There's another shipment coming..." she consulted the clipboard she held, "in five days. We'll either need more storage for them, or we'll have to drain that area over there." She pointed with the pen she held.

"We can't afford to waste a drop, so we'll pump it out faster. That might affect the taste, though. But what can we do?" Their voices faded as they neared the double doors. "I hope that cop won't be a problem. How the hell did they find those bodies…"

The doors closed behind them, leaving Rodriguez alone in the room. He swallowed back his horror as he went from bunk to bunk, snapping photos with his cell and sending them to Virgilio. As a secondary precaution, he also cc'd the Fresno Bee, the LA Times, and the New York Times.

"I'm sorry. It'll be over soon," he told the dehydrating bodies that surrounded him.

He made his way up to the offices and labs on the ground floor. Hydro-synth was not synthetic at all. Rodriguez could still hear the steady drip, drip, drip of body moisture plopping into the catch basins. He almost vomited when he thought about how much of this crap he'd eaten.

Well, no more, he thought as he laid the last of the wires in the main lab. It was ill conceived, what he planned, illegal and headstrong, but nowhere near as bad as what they were doing here. He'd hoped to get away, but he must have tripped an alarm. Guards poured into the room. He took shelter behind Andrew Cho's desk, his Magnum barking in response to their gunfire. He'd done what he could to let the world know what was happening here, the suffering so many had endured. His cousin's team would arrive in a few hours, the reporters had the story and photos. He'd done his part. It would end here, now. He grunted as a bullet pierced his shoulder. One to his chest slammed him against the wall. *I love you, Adrienne. I'm sorry*, he thought as with the last of his strength he reached out, pushed the plunger, and the Hydro-synth buildings exploded into rubble.

Susan's Fiction Books

Suspense
Tangled Webs
Sins of the Past
Piece By Piece
Death in the Valley

Paranormal Suspense
Proof of Identity

Historical Suspense
A Matter of Identity

Coming Soon:
Obsession, a novel of suspense
Stealing Shyon, an adult fantasy
The Skylark Series: paranormal detectives
Murder Under the Oaks (short story)
The Somewhen Murder (novella)
Dead Ringer (novella)

Someone Else's Eyes (novel)
Destany's Daughter, a paranormal YA/Adult
fantasy series
Demons Run series, a YA Fantasy

Susan's Nonfiction Books

Write It Right Workbooks (available from
Amazon Print) for fiction and creative
nonfiction writers of all levels:
Workbook #1: Units 1, 2, 3: Character, Setting,
Story
Workbook #2: Unit 4: POV,
Workbook #3: Units 5, 6: Plot, Dialogue
Workbook #4: Units 7, 8: Scenes, Style/Voice,
Conflict
Workbook #5: Units 9, 10: Conflict/Tension,
Subplot
Workbook #6: Units 11, 12: Beginnings,
Endings

Bonus Section: Novel Excerpts

Suspense Novels:
> *Tangled Webs*
> *Sins of the Past*
> *Piece By Piece*

Paranormal Suspense:
> *Proof of Identity*

Historical Suspense:
> *A Matter of Identity*

All of Susan's novels are available in print and Kindle format from Amazon.com. Print books can be ordered through any bookstore.

Tangled Webs

CHAPTER ONE

The perfect place, Lia thought, looking at the rustling chestnut trees beyond the wrought iron fence. *She can lie here and stare through the fence forever at the mansion she both coveted and resented, the people she both envied and hated. What could be better?*

She looked back down at the five-month-old grave, the earth half-settled with shy wisps of grass already poking out of the rich, dark soil, and read again the new inscription carved in an obviously old stone; a six-foot-deep rectangle of land bought years before with an eye to location. So typical.

Dorothea Willett
June 12, 1942—December 29, 2004
Disappointed in life, in family, in love
She never had a chance

Dorothea Willett.
Her mother.
Lia stood immobile, not even breathing, staring at the inscription and waiting to feel something,

anything. For so many years she'd wondered how she'd feel when this day finally came: anger, grief, relief, loss, spite, glee, indifference? She'd never once imagined she'd feel nothing, but that was what she felt. Nothing, not one thing, not even an infinitesimal flicker. It could have been a stranger lying beneath her feet. No, not even that, for a stranger would have engendered a vague sense of curiosity: how did she die, who was she, what kind of life had she had to leave an epitaph like that? But Lia stood filled with a blank unfeeling void. For ten minutes she stood, waiting for the dam to break, the other shoe to drop, the train to broadside her. Nothing happened.

Raising her brows she turned away with a sigh, made her way back down the hill, and turned right when she reached the main road, away from where she'd parked her car. She had just over an hour before the meeting with the lawyer where she would sign whatever needed signing and then get the hell out of there. She had no intention of staying one second longer than necessary, but as long as she was here she might as well sightsee. She certainly didn't want to hang around in the town.

I don't understand why I had to be here in person, she thought as she weaved her way between the tombstones, stopping to read one here and there, names echoing at her from the distant past. *There are notaries in Chicago, why couldn't he have just sent me what needed signing?*

Stumbling on the uneven ground, she put a hand on a reddish stone marker for balance. The unusual etching of a torch balanced on an open book caught her eye, and she paused to read the name. John

Lampland, the town librarian, had died four years ago. She remembered him fondly, he'd been so nice to her, one of the only ones who ever were. He'd seemed so old even back then that everyone said he'd live forever. Lia did the math and smiled to discover he'd reached ninety-seven just three days before his death. Knowing him, he was probably still shelving books when the Angels came to call.

She looked around then to get her bearings, and with a sinking feeling realized she was headed toward the stand of pines she remembered from so many years ago, another landmark she'd hoped never to see again. For a few seconds she considered heading back to the car, then she squared her shoulders and continued on her way. If she didn't go see it, she was afraid it would haunt her after she'd left. *Since I'm this close, I might as well head the ghosts off at the pass,* she told herself.

Not until she stood in the lee of the pines, the dirty white marker before her half-hidden by age, overgrowth and shadow, and felt her heart thud— once, twice—did she realize that deep inside she had hoped it wouldn't be here, that somehow someone would have moved it, moved him. *Idiot,* she said to herself, and then her eyes filled with tears of anger and self-pity. She felt the familiar, futile litany start: *Why me? What did I ever do to deserve him for a father?*

Dabney Willett, said the barely-legible chiseled words. Born in 1941, died—in a prison fight, two years into a life sentence for rape, torture and murder—in 1982. *Lived just long enough to make my life hell,* Lia thought, grinding the heels of her hands into her eyes to stop the tears. Though she knew it was hopeless, she couldn't stop herself from doing the math. He'd been

41 when a prison-made shiv pierced his heart. If he'd died at 30, there'd have been no rapes, no torture, no murders. Not so good for her, since she had to live with him, with them, but better for those young women who had died at his hands. If he'd died at 29, there would have been no Lia; definitely the solution she thought was best. Too bad old Dabney hadn't been nice enough to oblige her, and die before she'd been conceived. It would have made her life a whole lot easier.

I hate math, Lia thought as she turned away, then had to laugh at herself and her math degree. From a correspondence school, to be sure, but still a math degree. At least the fancy 'diploma' they'd sent said so, though she'd yet to find mathematical employment. So far she'd used her degree to subtract figures from her dwindling bank account, draft more quilt patterns than she could ever use, and figure out ages from tombstones. It amazed her that she was so good at something she hated. She laughed again to herself; sometimes life's little ironies just tickled her funny bone.

She stood a moment by the side of the road, soaking up the sun's warmth, breathing in the heady scent of clover and new-mown grass. Bees droned past on endless errands; birds twittered and sang in the hushed stillness. She glanced at her watch; still forty long minutes to kill. *Time sure flies when you're having fun*, she thought, rolling her eyes, then turned her reluctant steps toward the pond. She'd known this visit was inevitable ever since she'd read the attorney's letter and realized she'd have to tread where she'd sworn she never would again.

I should have studied ghost busting, she thought, shuddering as she spotted the grave, guarded now by an elaborate stone memorial featuring a slender young woman in stone shorts and halter top, half-recumbent in the bow of a small boat. Sweet longing graced the statue's lovely face; granite eyes gazed with fathomless emotion at the softly rippling water of the picturesque, kidney shaped pond where ducks and swans floated a zigzag course among reeds and lily pads, looking for handouts.

The statue headstone hadn't been there the last —the only—time Lia'd been to the grave. She was amazed at how much it looked like Cerise. The sculptor must have had pictures to work from. It was so lifelike, Lia almost expected it to come alive, to step out of the boat and down from the pedestal and drive her into the ground with mocking laughter just like Cerise used to do. The vision suddenly was too real; Lia couldn't breathe. Blinking, she jerked back a couple of steps and fought air into her lungs as she wrested her gaze from the frozen face. By the time her heartbeat had slowed down and she could breathe normally again, she found herself staring at the words cut deep into the base of the monument.

Cerise Gayle Forrester
March 11, 1970 – September 21, 1987
Beloved Daughter
Devoted Sister
Loyal Friend
Lost to the seas she loved so much

Lia had no need to do any math; these statistics were burned into her brain years ago. Cerise had been seventeen when she'd fallen off her boat, hit her head and drowned. Fresh from a wild party and then a fight with her father and alone on a stormy lake in the wee hours of the morning in a boat with a dead engine, an engine that showed signs of having been tampered with. Though nothing could ever be proven, suspicion had settled on the most obvious suspect, the one with a murderer's blood in her veins. Like father, like daughter, they all whispered, and suspicion hardened into conviction. But though her memories of that time were still fragmented, Lia knew one thing for certain. She'd had nothing to do with Cerise's untimely death.

"What really happened that night, Cerise?" she whispered, unable to tear her gaze from the death date chiseled into the stone. "Who did this to you?"

She stood caught in a nightmare past, a place of vague shadow and dark confusion, unbearable pain and formless terror. It stalked her, a clinging ebony miasma that threatened to devour her, to drown her as surely as Cerise had drowned—

A crow screeched overhead and Lia jumped, pulled abruptly from the dark past. Blinking, she shook her head to clear the fog and cobwebs, then wrapped her arms around her shivering body. Her watch glinted in the sunlight, and when she checked the dial she realized it was time to start for the lawyer's office.

"Goodbye, Cerise," she said, giving the statue one last uneasy glimpse before she turned back to retrace her steps to her car. The flint-hard eyes kept their gaze on the sun-dappled water. The stone lips still held their tiny, cruel curve.

Oh yeah, that's Cerise, all right, Lia thought as she walked down the cemetery's main road. *Beautiful, cold and cruel.* More than ever, she couldn't wait to leave this town, and its unwanted memories, far behind her once again.

As she approached a hedge-screened crossroad, a man suddenly appeared, tall, broad-shouldered, striding along with his hands deep in his pockets, his head of wavy, sand-colored hair bent down in silent contemplation. He swung into the main road and continued on in the direction Lia'd come from, unaware of their near-collision. Lia swerved and went past him before recognition burst upon her. She gasped and turned, a tentative smile on her lips.

"Cord?"

The man stopped and turned to look. He shook his head then frowned and walked back to within a few feet of her. His icy blue eyes, glaring hatred and contempt, dropped the length of her body and back up again, and Lia felt her smile slowly vanish.

"My God, it is you. I don't believe it."

The low growl pierced her like an arrow, and Lia blinked, taken aback at the depth of his emotion.

"Well," she swallowed back the pain and almost managed to smile at him again, "it's good to see you, too, Cord."

"What the hell are you doing here?"

"Just here on business." Lia shrugged. "Legal business."

"Oh. Yeah, I heard about your Mother." Cord glanced toward the rise on which Dorothea was buried, then narrowed his eyes at Lia. "I hope you're not thinking of waxing nostalgic and sticking around here for any length of time. You're not welcome, you know. In fact, it could be downright dangerous for you."

"Oh, don't worry about that." Hurt and anger roughened Lia's voice. "I have no intention of staying here one second longer than I have to."

"That suits me just fine."

They stared at each other, the tension between them so thick it was almost visible. Finally, Lia closed her eyes, shook her head and in a pained sigh let go the breath she hadn't been aware of holding.

"Still so bitter, Cord? It's been seventeen years. Shouldn't you have put it behind you by now?"

"Put it behind me? After what you did?"

"I didn't do anything."

"Bullshit! Your fingerprints were in the boat, on the engine—"

"So were about fifty others. Marshall gave everyone rides that night."

"But you were the one who fought with her, beat her up—"

"Beat her up? Are you crazy? All I did was throw my sandals at her. I couldn't stand it, she took you away from me."

"I was never yours!"

"Yes, you were! And you betrayed me. With her! It hurt so much, I thought I'd die."

"I wish you had!" Cord's hands curled into fists. "It should have been you. But it was Cerise, *Cerise* who died."

"Not because of anything I did."

"I know it was you."

"It was not."

"You always hated her."

"Not as much as she hated me!"

They stood panting, glaring at each other in the cathedral-like stillness, oblivious of the surrounding headstones, the honeyed warmth of the sun, the traffic passing on the street beyond the wrought iron fence. Finally, Cord took a step closer to her, raised his fist a few inches. Lia tensed, wondering if he would hit her. Again. When he spoke, he snarled his words slow and clear, as if to grind them into her very soul.

"It is your fault she's dead. Everyone knows it. Even if you didn't tamper with the boat, she was out on that lake because of you."

Lia blinked; her mouth dropped open, and she uttered a short, astounded laugh.

"And how do you figure that?"

"You said you'd make her sorry, and you did. You knew she was grounded. You called her father and told him she'd snuck out to the party."

"No. I didn't."

"Liar!"

"Cord, I did *not* call Mr. Forrester. I *never* called Mr. Forrester."

Cord gloated, a nasty little smile on his lips. "He said you did. You told him who you were."

"Oh, for God's sake, Cord!" Lia threw her hands up in exasperation. "Mr. Forrester barely knew me, he would never have recognized my voice. Anyone could have called him and said it was me, he wouldn't have known the difference." Cord merely stared at her, his steel-hard eyes confirming his disbelief of her argument. "Listen, do you really think that if I'd called him, I'd have been stupid enough to give him my name?"

"Why not? You were stupid enough to come back here, weren't you?"

Abruptly, all emotion drained from Lia. Nothing had changed, nothing would ever change. It had all died seventeen years ago, along with Cerise Forrester.

"Goodbye, Cord."

She turned away. He grabbed her right arm, pulled her back a step, then reached out his free hand to her face, touched the faint scars etched beside her left eye and along her cheekbone. Startled, Lia jerked her face away from his fingers. Cord's eyes softened; a frown creased his brow. He let go of her arm.

"Did I do that?" he asked in an almost disbelieving tone.

Swallowing against an assault of painful memories and the guilt in Cord's eyes, Lia could not trust her voice. All she could do was nod, once.

Cord stared at her a moment longer, then his eyes hardened again and his face lit up with a self-satisfied smile.

"Good."

He turned and strode away without a backward glance, leaving Lia anchored in a sea of shock and pain.

When at last she could move, she stumbled the rest of the way to her car, her vision almost blocked by nightmares from the past. She sat behind the wheel for more than five minutes before the onslaught of memories faded and her hands steadied enough to fit the keys into the ignition. The depth of Cord's hatred seared her. She hadn't thought it possible for anyone to hate like that. Rubbing her hands over her face to banish the last wisps of the past, she turned the key and put the car in drive.

All I want is to get out of here, she thought as she exited the cemetery. *Please, just get me out of here.*

Proof of Identity

(an indieB.R.A.G. Medallion awardee)

CHAPTER ONE
BUFFALO, NEW YORK
SEPTEMBER, 1986

Death was the furthest thing from her mind. She sat on the blanket and watched Trey walk toward the Lamborghini, his broad shoulders back, blond head held high, stride sure and ground-eating—a man on a mission. She still couldn't believe she was here with Carleton Andrews III, aka Trey: Triple-degreed and pedigreed; movie-star gorgeous and filthy rich; a mover and shaker in the world of high finance. He owned a fifty-foot yacht, his own jet and a huge mansion in Buffalo, New York, as well as a lofty condo in Manhattan and a chateau in Paris. And he had deigned to notice her, Danae Holloway, a lowly typist in an investment firm, who'd gone to secretarial school instead of college and who didn't even own a rust bucket car, much less a three-hundred-thousand dollar piece of extravagance. She

still wasn't sure how it had happened, how a simple offer of a ride home had led to this fairy-tale love story.

Trey opened the Lamborghini's trunk and Danae turned to look out at the Niagara River. The swift current carried with it a sense of urgency, tension belied by the inviting coolness of the grass where she sat and the casual fluttering of maple leaves on the scattered trees. She rubbed her hands over her face, gently massaging the lingering soreness around her eyes, a vestige from the latest headache attack.

She'd come to dread those headaches. The excruciating pain now carried with it a surreal quality. Misty visions obscured her sight. Sounds reverberated through her body. The changes terrified her. She couldn't stop worrying about a brain tumor, or something equally horrible, even though all the tests had come back negative. They were, according to the doctors, just headaches. Terrible headaches that presaged a few days of suffering and nothing else. She hoped.

And now there was Trey.

Please, she thought, *if I'm sleeping, I don't ever want to wake up.*

It made her nervous, being this happy. She had coasted for so long being vaguely content; all her life, really. She'd never even looked for true happiness. It hadn't occurred to her she was eligible for it. She still wasn't sure what she had done to deserve this turn of events, and so she found it hard to believe in it. To believe that it was real, that it would last. To believe it was hers.

"Have you recovered yet from meeting the old *pater familias*?"

Trey's tall, strong body blocked out the sun as his deep, resonant voice showered down on her. Danae looked up and smiled at him.

"It wasn't nearly as bad as I feared it would be. Though you're right, he is terribly intimidating. But underneath it he's a nice man. Really nice. I like him, and I think he liked me." She let her voice wander up into a half-question, seeking confirmation from Trey.

"Well, since he didn't snap your head off or eat you or anything, I'd say that's a safe bet." Trey dropped down on the blanket. "Wedding books from Meredith," he said, handing her a half-dozen magazines. "And champagne."

"You're spoiling me," Danae said. She opened *Today's Bride* as Trey worked on the cork.

"Forever and always." The cork popped from the bottle and they laughed. "Meredith said she marked the best stuff for you. Take a look." He turned away to pour the bubbly wine into two crystal glasses.

"She did?" Danae flipped to the first marked page and her heart sank. "That's nice of her."

"You don't sound so sure, my love." Danae looked up and Trey fed her a caviar hors d'oeuvres. "What's wrong?"

Danae shook her head as she chewed, then swallowed the caviar.

"Nothing, Trey, not really. But I don't think your sister likes me very much. I'm not sure I'm comfortable with her planning our wedding."

"Nonsense, darling. She might be a bit curt, but that's just her way. Trust me. If I love you, she loves you too. And she'll make sure ours is the wedding of the century. They'll spend years trying to outdo us."

"If you say so. But," Danae looked down at the open magazine, "me in this? I don't think so."

Trey looked at the picture of a model buried beneath yards of frilly tulle and ribbons of multicolored pastel hues, and burst out laughing. "Good God, that looks like a Halloween costume! That can't be one of Meredith's choices."

He took the magazine from her and flipped the page. "Ah, see? You were looking at the wrong side. Now, this is more like it." He handed the magazine back to Danae. "Vera Wang. Meredith says she's the best. And you'd be the proverbial dream walking in this one. It's perfect. My personal favorite." He waggled his brows at her.

"Um." Danae bit her lip as she gazed at the sophisticated, high-fashion gown sprinkled with pearls and rhinestones. "It's strapless. And backless. And so short."

"Only in front." He gave her a smug grin. "It's long in the back."

"But it's not me, Trey. I don't think I could wear that." Danae turned a few pages and stopped at an unmarked one that featured a floor-length, silk Victorian-style gown with understated embroidery around the hem. "Oh. Now this is lovely. It's just what I want."

"Never. It's too plain, too..." Trey shuddered. "Ugh. No, don't protest, my love." He placed his fingers on her lips to stop her words. "I know more about this than you do, even if I am just a man. We Andrews' have a certain image to uphold, you know. I was right about your outfit today, wasn't I? Aren't you glad I made you go back and change?"

"I guess," Danae said, still not sure what was wrong with the lilac cotton sweater and white slacks she'd originally had on. If she were honest about it, she'd felt a bit overdressed in the black and white silk shell and black linen skirt Trey had bought her and insisted she wear. It seemed their ideas about casual clothing were totally different. Trey's father had seemed to appreciate the outfit, though.

"You'll be gorgeous in this gown," Trey said, though Danae feared she would feel—and look – like she was playing dress-up in it. "Don't look so worried about it, my love. By the time the wedding rolls around next spring, Meredith and I will have you totally made over. You won't recognize yourself."

He caressed her face, then pulled her forward and captured her lips with his. His tongue played with hers, then he shivered kisses onto her cheeks, her chin, down her neck. Her body melted beneath his touch and her breath caught in her throat. He laid her back on the blanket and slid his mouth to her ear.

"Just follow Meredith's advice and you'll be the perfect bride," he whispered, "the perfect wife. Leave it all up to her. She has the bridesmaids picked out, seven I think, and the reception booked. We'll have three or four hundred of our closest friends—"

Danae gasped and pushed Trey away.

"Three or four *hundred*? But I thought we agreed it would be a small ceremony."

"That *is* small. Denton had thirteen hundred at his wedding." Trey sat up and frowned. "This is what I want, Danae. This will make me happy. You in the dress I love, with my closest friends around us. Don't you want me to be happy?"

Danae sat up and smoothed her fingers over the crease between his eyes. She'd known from the beginning that they came from two different worlds, and if a compromise was needed it would have to come from her. She was moving into his world, after all, not him into hers. It would mean learning a new way of thinking, of talking, of dressing and entertaining. Servants and chauffeurs, charity events and even rubbing elbows with royalty at times. It was a lifestyle of which she had no real conception. Trey was right. If she didn't let Meredith teach her, remake her, she would never fit in. She would be an embarrassment to Trey, and she could never do that to him.

But that dress... it would be an embarrassment to her. And she wasn't sure she was ready to give up all of herself. At least not yet.

"As much as you want me to be happy," she said. "Maybe even more. So, here's what I propose." Trey's brows beetled and she again smoothed away the crease. "Meredith can have carte blanche with everything but the dress, you can invite the whole world if you want, and I'll pick out the gown. No," she answered his frowned question, "not the Victorian one, I can see you don't like it, but not that strapless, backless one, either. Whatever I choose, I promise you'll love every inch of it."

"You don't like the Vera Wang even a little?" Trey pouted like a three-year-old, his eyes stormy, his arms crossed over his chest.

"I..." Danae's stomach clenched as she tried to find words that wouldn't come.

"Never mind." Trey laid a gentle hand on her cheek, but his eyes still held a *soupçon* of annoyance. "Don't try to appease me. The lie will just make you sick."

"I'm sorry, Trey. Forgive me? Please?" He turned his head, stared out at the glittering water. Danae ran her fingertip down his arm. "I'll be beautiful. Really. I promise."

"Okay." Trey heaved a deep sigh. "Fine. Have it your way. But I'm upping the guest list." He shook his head, then pursed his lips and turned to her. Amazement spread across his face. "Did you just con me into a compromise?"

Danae shrugged and grinned at him. Trey threw his head back and laughed.

"You little vixen. My god, I love you," he said. He picked up the champagne glasses and handed one to her. "To us and a long life together."

Danae smiled, clinked glasses and sipped the wine, wrinkling her nose at the bubbles. She could do this, she just needed time. It had happened so fast, they'd only met in July. Just over two months of whirlwind. She'd barely had time to think, much less assimilate any lessons or change her way of doing things. But she was learning. She'd find something he'd love that she could wear if she killed herself looking. This time she'd not fail to please, even if it meant becoming someone different. Someone who one day might wear a strapless, backless dress. She'd make Trey proud. She'd be exactly what he wanted—

"Oh!"

Something shiny glittered in the dregs of her wine. She fished it out and gasped.

"I told you I'd get you one," Trey said, taking the ring from her hand and sliding it on her left ring finger. It fit perfectly. "Do you like it?"

"It's gorgeous," she breathed, afraid if she blinked it would vanish. The pear-shaped diamond glittered in the late afternoon sun. Tiny ruby clusters at each side threw narrow red slashes onto the white in her blouse. "I've never seen anything so beautiful. Or big."

"Three carats. Only the best for my love."

She laughed and kissed him.

"I can't wait to show Sandie. And everyone at the office. They'll be so excited for us."

"Danae," Trey laid a warm hand on her shoulder, "we've talked about this. You can't tell anyone, not until after the engagement party. Please. Meredith's worked so hard on it, we can't spoil it for her."

"But it's so hard, Trey. I'm so happy, I want to share it with everyone."

"And you will, my love. In a few weeks." He kissed her. "We'll have a whole lifetime together. What do a few weeks matter?" He kissed her again. "Okay?"

"Okay," she sighed, knowing it was again her turn to compromise.

They lingered until almost sunset, drinking champagne, eating pate and caviar, and planning their life together while Danae hoped she could become what Trey wanted her to be. She'd so rarely been able to please her father, though she'd tried her best, always. Now she determined to work twice as hard to be what Trey needed her to be. She just couldn't fail again, not this time.

They left the park and Trey insisted she turn the diamond around so it nestled in her palm. He kissed her breathless when he dropped her off at her apartment, but when she set off for the grocery store a few minutes later she turned the ring back around so that it fractured the light from the street lamps. She couldn't help grinning as she walked the four blocks to the store. She wanted to stop everyone she passed and babble out the news before she burst. She didn't know how she was going to keep it a secret from her co-workers, never mind Sandie to whom she told everything.

She stopped just inside the supermarket entrance. At this late hour only one checkout was open. *I could show the checkout woman*, Danae thought. *She doesn't even know me. How could it hurt for her to see it?* Then Trey's words echoed in her head: please, don't tell anyone until after the party. She realized this was her first loyalty test. If she couldn't pass it, she had no business marrying Carleton Andrews, III. Danae took a deep breath, turned the diamond into her palm, picked up milk, bread, eggs, tomatoes and cat food, and merely smiled at the cashier. She walked home hugging her secret to herself.

She glanced at her upper window as she turned up her front walk. Pandora stood on the couch back, front paws scrabbling at the glass. Danae could see the animal's mouth gape and knew the cat was shrieking her displeasure.

"I'm coming, I'm coming," Danae said. "Spoiled brat. You're not even out of food yet."

The cat reared up and smacked the glass with both front paws. Danae shook her fist at the feline.

"You break it, you fix it, Bratella," Danae called as the cat leapt down from the window ledge and vanished. "Better work on growing those opposable thumbs we talked about."

Danae started up the porch steps, laughing to herself. It sure would be interesting to see how Trey's greyhound and her cat got along—if anyone or anything could get along with Pandora.

"Miss Holloway? Danae Holloway?"

The deep, raspy voice stilled her feet halfway up the steps. She turned and looked behind her. Two men stood on the bottom step, one short and slender, the other a massive hulk with jutting nose and chin. Halfway down the walk stood another man covered in shadow. Danae's heart skipped a beat.

"Yes. I'm Danae," she said.

The huge man came up two more steps until his head was even with hers. Danae caught movement at the corner of her eye. She looked back at the porch. A fourth man moved out of the darkness to stand blocking her way to the porch deck, pale eyes guarded, brown hair gleaming in the light over the front door. He stood alert, legs spread, arms slightly bent at the elbows. Alarm skittered along her nerves.

"Miss Holloway." The deep voice turned her back to the large man on the steps. "My name is Carter. Lieutenant Walt Carter. These men are my detectives. You're under arrest, Miss Holloway, for the murder of John Bauer."

Sins of the Past

CHAPTER ONE

Mitch Lawson read through the last two files yet another time, sighing aloud and hoping for lightning to strike. Nothing happened. Whatever was amiss wouldn't come clear. Growling, he kneaded the bridge of his substantial nose. *This wouldn't have happened a few years ago*, he thought, shoving files aside. *This goddamn pencil-pushing, paper-rattling, desk-jockey job is killing me.*

He snorted in disgust and glared at the nameplate perched on the edge of the dark mahogany desk: Mitchell James Lawson, Coordinating Liaison. Him, a bureaucrat, for pity's sake. Once the Marshal Service's top field agent, Mister too-valuable-to-be-pensioned-off Lawson now slowly lost his mind in the Freaking Bureaucracy of Idiots, collating facts and figures for the National Incident-Based Reporting System (NIBRS). Nothing but busy work tailor-made for the company screw-up. He wasn't a real agent, he was a paper agent. A paper agent in a paper city in a paper world. He'd like to strangle the bastard who invented the frigging stuff.

He wanted to be a Marshal still, not an FBI bureaucrat. He wanted to be out on the streets not in a paneled office. With his .357 magnum where it belonged, snugged beneath his armpit, not stuffed in a drawer. He wanted the danger back, the excitement, the anticipation of the unknown. What did he have to look forward to here? Eye strain? Paper cuts?

It's your own fault, buck-o, he reminded himself, glaring at the miniature Alp of folders on his desk, his punishment for taking two weeks off. *You're the one who screwed up. You misread the situation, not someone else. You played it wrong and got shot for your efforts. No one to blame here but yourself.* The proof was in his daily life—hours of safe, dull, boring work in a safe, dull, boring office.

And now his elephantine memory had holes in it.

He shook his head. Maybe a break would help. Mitch growled again and shoved away from the desk. He thrust himself out of his chair and turned toward the window. Pain shot up his left side from knee to hip. His leg buckled and he stumbled up against the desk. Like a churning mudslide, the mountain of files cascaded onto the gray carpeting, sweeping nameplate and pencil holder with them. Grimacing, he stood massaging the pain in his hip, shaking his head and staring at the mess littering the floor. *Can it get any better than this?* he asked himself as he waited for the pain to abate. *Can it just fucking get any better?*

The door opened and his secretary, Kelsey of the velvet voice and fuck-me heels, wiggle-hipped across the carpet. She set a steaming cup of the decaffeinated, half-herbal brew she deemed coffee on the newly cleared desk. She looked down at the file-strewn floor and shook her head.

"Mr. Lawson. What happened here?"

Mitch shrugged. "Earthquake."

"Funny, I didn't feel anything."

Mitch grunted.

"It epicentered on me."

"So I see." Kelsey smiled and stooped to retrieve the folders.

"You don't have to do that."

"I know, I just can't help myself. It's a conditioned response, like Pavlov's dogs salivating." Kelsey handed Mitch a stack of folders, which he set on the glossy desktop. Then she reached for more. "The price of having kids."

"My sister's the same way," Mitch said, shuddering slightly at the way Kelsey's voice stroked down his tingling nerves. She knew exactly what the sound of her voice did to most men, and he knew she used it to her advantage. That she was also one of the most efficient, intelligent secretaries he'd ever met, was for Mitch mere icing on the cake. "She's always wiping or picking up something, no matter who drops it. And cutting up everyone's food. Thank God I dodged that bullet."

"There are rewards, you know." Kelsey stood up, put the last of the files on the desk and looked at Mitch, who took a step back.

"No, I don't. And I don't want to. I am quite content being a carefree bachelor, thank you very much."

"And using Maureen's boys as surrogate kids. Best of both worlds, huh?"

"Absolutely," Mitch said. He winked and moved to the window, hoping, as he opened the blinds to the rain-swept dusk, that his slight limp wasn't noticeable. He might have ended a mere desk jockey, shuffled over to the FBI, but he'd be damned if he'd show any of the weakness that had caused his fall from grace.

"What I came in for, Mr. Lawson, is to remind you that it's getting late. Are you leaving anytime soon? Or are you going to ruin the entire value of your vacation in one day?"

"No, and yes," Mitch said, looking out at the rain-blurred lights.

"I thought so." In the window's reflection, Mitch watched Kelsey cross her arms, tilt her head and study him, her auburn locks a fiery contrast to his sand-colored hair. "Is there any possible way I can make you go home at a reasonable hour?"

"Only if you promise to come with me and talk to me all night. You know how I love your voice. For relaxing, it's even better than that Bahamian beach." Mitch turned and grinned at her. "Pure heaven."

"If I come, my five-year-old will have to come with me. And he never shuts up—he even talks in his sleep. You'd never hear a word I'd say."

Mitch shook his head. "You're a hard woman, Kelsey McGuire. You should be kinder to me, considering my advanced age."

Kelsey laughed and Mitch almost purred with pleasure. "Nonsense. Forty-seven is the prime of life, Mr. Lawson. And I don't believe," she picked up the coffee cup and walked over to give it to him, "that you went to any Bahamian beach. I think you went to Ireland and kissed the Blarney Stone—again."

Mitch chuckled. He set the cup on the window ledge and turned to watch the city outside glimmer through the rain into an iridescent sheen as full dark fell, absently twisting his onyx ring round and round on his finger.

"Look at that, Kelsey. Isn't it amazing? So beautiful."

"Like an enchanted fairyland wrapped in velvet," Kelsey murmured.

"You know," Mitch sighed, "I think I'll miss this the most when my time comes, the way the city lights up at night. Those lights look like warm glowing jewels. Or beacons of hope maybe. An oasis of welcome in a cold and indifferent world."

Mitch fell silent, his mind wandering back to the file that had caught him up short. Kelsey looked up at him, her face solemn. Mitch frowned and shook his head.

"But there weren't any welcoming beacons that day," he said. "No comforting, man-made incandescence, not on a sunny summer afternoon. A hell of a time to die, wasn't it, when everything else was so alive? Odd that Webster didn't detail the stolen items, the things the guy died for—"

Mitch froze, his recalcitrant memory finally displaying the appropriate pages to his mind's eye. A premonitory shiver went down his spine. He could hear the traffic on the street below, feel the thud of his own heart, as again he saw the victim's name, the impersonal, abbreviated description of the crime, the lack of evidence that had quickly stymied the local police investigation. He scanned Agent Webster's oh-so-logical conclusion. Another innocent victim unfortunate enough to be home at the wrong time. Logical, yes. But wrong. Dead wrong, if Mitch's memory hadn't totally failed him. And it hadn't. Though it had been years, he knew damn well that it hadn't.

"Mr. Lawson?" Kelsey asked, frowning. "Is everything all right?"

Mitch whirled and strode to the desk, shoving files around until he found the one he wanted. Then he turned and pointed at Kelsey.

"Don't leave until I get back," he ordered. "And don't let Dan Jeffers leave, either. I'm going to need him."

He left her staring open-mouthed at his retreating back and took the stairs up two flights to the Bureau Chief's office. Mrs. Marlin, Oscar Henry's sixty-something martinet of a personal assistant, stood up as Mitch thrust open the office suite door.

"Is he still in?" Mitch asked, not slowing to hear her response. He could see light behind the frosted glass panel in the door to the Chief's office.

"You can't go in there, Mr. Lawson," Mrs. Marlin grated in her two-pack-a-day voice. "He's in a meeting. Mr. Lawson. Stop!"

Mitch didn't break stride. He moved down the short hall and shouldered his way into the inner sanctum. Ignoring the man sitting in the visitor's chair, he marched up to the Chief's desk and dropped the file, open to the pertinent page, in front of Oscar Henry.

"Yes, it's all right, Mrs. Marlin," Henry said into the phone, his deep voice gentle and soothing. He glared at Mitch. "I certainly cannot expect you to stop a runaway train. I will deal with it. You go on home and we'll talk about it in the morning."

Henry dropped the receiver on the cradle and held up a finger when Mitch started to speak. He gave the page a cursory scan and raised angry, deep-charcoal eyes to Mitch's face. "You remember Joe Islington, don't you, Mitchell?" Henry waited until the two men shook hands, then turned to Islington. "Will you excuse us a minute, Joe? I need to hand this young man his head."

Smiling, Islington nodded, stood and quietly left the room.

"Oscar," Mitch said, but Henry cut him off with a gesture as elegant and sophisticated as his attire. It was hard to believe he'd once been a defensive tackle for the NFL.

"What makes you think you can barge in here whenever you want, Lawson?" Only the raised pitch of Henry's normally soft, drawling voice attested to his anger. "I don't know how you did things in the Marshal Service, but here there are rules. And they apply to you, too. You need to calm down and follow protocol. Do you think Islington won't take the tale of your impertinence back to the White House? I have enough to deal with, without adding failure to control my employees into the mix."

Mitch, despite the urge to kowtow in the face of the Chief's disapproval, leaned on the desk and shoved the file closer to Henry. "It's one of mine, Oscar," he said, his voice filled with fury and pain. "From the Program. This shouldn't have happened. Go on, read it. And then tell me to calm down."

He paced while Henry, his thick, strong fingers turning pages in their methodical way, read through the file. At last he looked up at Mitch and nodded.

"This is disturbing, to say the least. How long has he been—"

"Fifteen years."

"And how long since you last—"

"Eleven years."

"You're sure it was—"

"Yes, I'm sure. And so are you. We both know who did this." Mitch ran his hand through his hair and growled. "He was well hidden. It shouldn't have happened!"

"These people have long memories," Henry reminded Mitch. "Nothing is ever forgotten, or forgiven. Have you any idea how he was found?"

"Not yet, but I will," Mitch growled, his eyes flashing. "That Webster is an idiot!"

"Cut the boy some slack. He was working without the insider information you have." Henry closed his eyes a moment, then nodded. "I'll assign Lacey and Parrett to the follow-up. They're two of my best."

"No!" Mitch whirled and leaned over the desk, suppressing a grimace as pain again flared in his leg. Startled, Henry raised his brows. "This is my case, Oscar. I'll do the follow-up. Give me two weeks and Dan Jeffers—"

"No. You are not a Marshal anymore. And you're not a field agent, Mitchell."

"I'm still better than those two put together, Oscar, and you know it. Just one week—"

"Absolutely not. You don't have status."

"This is my case, damn it!"

"Not anymore. Protocol states—"

"Fuck protocol!" Mitch spat.

"Mr. Lawson," Henry intoned, his hardened voice one of warning. He began to rise, his huge dark palms pressing on the desktop. Mitch held up his hands and struggled to contain his anger. He shook his head, stepped back to lean beside the window and crossed his arms. The Chief subsided to watch Mitch through narrowed eyes.

"I'm sorry, Oscar. That was out of line." Mitch looked up to see Henry incline his head, accepting the apology. "But damn it, this is personal. It's my case, has been from day one. *I* coached him, *I* made sure they placed him well, *I* promised he'd be safe. And now he's dead." The muscles in Mitch's jaw worked as he ground his teeth. "I *have* to do the follow-up, Oscar. I *need* to do it." Mitch glanced out the window, frowning, his voice pinched from more than just physical pain. "I have to know if it was me, if I screwed up again, if did something that let him be found, even after all this time."

Henry cleared his throat. "I very much doubt you did, Mitchell. You were too good at your job to make a mistake about something so important."

"Yeah, right," Mitch muttered, the muscles in his jaw working.

Henry waited a beat before continuing.

"It was probably one of a thousand things you had no hand in, or control over."

Mitch lifted one shoulder.

"Maybe. But I have to know. Do you understand, Oscar? I have to find out or it'll haunt me. Destroy me. And don't tell me I'll get a copy of the report. Lacey and Parrett could overlook a clue or misinterpret evidence. I'm the only one who can do this because I'm the only one who knows it all—both what's in the original file, and what isn't. Not even the other Marshals know it all."

Henry shook his head. Mitch gave him a grim smile, seeing the denial in the Chief's face. He straightened up, looked Oscar Henry in the eyes.

"The follow-up, Oscar. Please. Let me do it with official sanction."

"You'd do it without?" Henry sounded surprised.

"If you force me."

Mitch waited while Henry studied the determination he knew was etched in his eyes, his face, his whole body. After a long moment Henry sighed and nodded.

"I'll give you two days, Mitchell," he said. "That's all."

"I need more than two, Oscar."

"Really? Lacey and Parrett could do it in two, and you just told me that you're better than both of them put together. Is that not correct?"

Mitch heaved an irritated sigh and crossed his arms.

"You're enjoying this, aren't you?" he growled.

Henry's lips twitched. "What about Dan Jeffers?"

"Only if it's absolutely necessary. He has his own work to do. And I want a full report on this from you at lunch on Thursday. One o'clock. Don't be late. We'll review your sorry excuse for a budget at that time, also. And Lawson," he added as Mitch turned away from the desk. Mitch paused but didn't turn around. "Don't ever back me into a corner again. You will find it most unpleasant when I come out fighting. And I will, you can bet on that. Once has always been my limit."

Mitch turned his head and nodded his understanding. Not until he'd crossed the room and his hand was on the doorknob did the Chief speak again.

"On your way out, wake Joe Islington and send him back in here, will you? The White House is waiting for my answer. And you owe Mrs. Marlin an apology for your rudeness—an abject one, asap. It would be prudent not to wait until morning. I think flowers would be a nice addition."

"Understood, Chief," Mitch said, smiling.

He'd lost the smile by the time he entered his office suite and dropped the file on Kelsey's desk.

"Jeffers?" he asked. "We've got work to do."

"Waiting in your office," she said, and blinked at him. "I see you got what you wanted."

"Yep. But I owe Mrs. Marlin some flowers. I hope there's a florist still open."

Kelsey grinned and shook her head. Picking up a pen, Mitch jotted notes on a piece of scratch paper from her desk and handed it to her.

"Pull those files before you leave, Kelsey. And order something in for Jeffers and me, it's going to be a long night. Make it Italian, lots of cheese. The hell with my arteries. And I'll need to talk to the idiot who wrote up that file, what's his name, Webster? I'd like to know who trained him, he's a poor excuse for a field agent. Then make a reservation on the first flight out tomorrow—no, tonight if possible—and get me full background on the local-yokel detective in charge of this case. Let's hope he's got more intelligence than our boy's shown. Call them both after you make the plane reservation and let them know when I'll get there." He took a deep breath and raked a hand through his hair. "Unless I'm very much mistaken, the sins of the past finally caught up with this one. And the payment sure wasn't pretty."

Piece By Piece

CHAPTER ONE
October 14, 1987
Harrisburg, Pa.

The phone's scream shattered the silence and sent Ogden Wilkes' pulse racing. He hated the anemic electronic beeps that passed for telephone bells nowadays, though his pounding heart wouldn't have minded one now, at ten after four in the morning.

He reached out and snared the receiver before he opened his eyes, not wanting his wife to wake, though he knew Judy couldn't sleep through even one shrill ring. It was a game they played. He grabbed the receiver as quickly as he could so she could sleep on, and she lay with her back to him, eyes wide and heart thudding, he was sure, pretending she had not heard. It allowed him to leave the house with a minimum of fuss. And it allowed her to roll over and mumble at him, questions that did not touch on the reasons for the untimely calls. He knew the only way Judy could accept the dangerous work he did in daylight was not to acknowledge why her husband was called out of bed at night. Ogden Wilkes respected that, which was why he played the game.

"Yes, what is it?" he said now in a low tone, though he already knew. Only the murder of someone big or the wounding of one of his men would drag the precinct Captain out of his warm bed. He inched himself up against the padded headboard, trying not to shake the mattress. Musuko, who slept on the floor under the partially open window, sat up, head cocked, ears aquiver, front paws restless on the soft carpeting.

"Traynor here, Captain. I'm with Snelling in an alley near the river, between Fourth and Lexington. I think you'd better get down here."

Through the static from the squad car mic, Wilkes could hear a jumbled commotion in the background.

"Who is it?" He threw back the covers, swung his feet to the floor.

"Cliff Davisson."

"Channel Three's reporter?" Wilkes glanced at his wife's stiff back. "Who found him?"

"A couple on their way home from a bar. She needed to puke, they cut down the alley."

"You first on scene?"

Traynor paused. Wilkes ground his teeth. Then Traynor gave a sharp sigh.

"Almost. Abernathy caught the squeal on patrol, beat me by maybe five minutes."

"We need to contain this, Bill," Wilkes growled. "You know that."

"Yes. I'm on it, sir."

"OK. Ten minutes. No one goes near him until I get there, including the lab boys."

"Yes, sir."

Wilkes rubbed his eyes. It took ever-greater will power to motivate his forty-seven-year-old body to start a day at four a.m. But there was no help for it. The popular TV reporter's murder would spread ripples of shock and righteous indignation throughout the entire community. If Wilkes were not to be buried in the fallout, he'd have to supervise every step of this investigation personally.

He rose, took up the clothes laid out on the chair beside the bed and went into the bathroom to dress. Glancing in the mirror, he rasped a hand over the dark stubble on his chin and decided not to shave. It would enhance his image of dedication to be caught in disarray by news hounds' flashbulbs—hot from his bed and indifferent to his own grooming in the face of tragedy. He growled with annoyed exasperation that he knew would only grow as the hours and days passed. This one would be a ball-breaker, front-page news all the way.

Judy turned over and stretched her arms over her head when he reentered the bedroom.

"What is it, Ogden?"

"It's nothing, go back to sleep." He crossed to the bed and kissed her cheek. She didn't open her eyes. "Just a little trouble down at the station. Don't worry about breakfast, I'll pick up something downtown."

"Um-hmmm," she mumbled, turning back onto her side. The streetlight shining in through the window silvered her pale hair. Her lashes cast long shadow-streaks down her plump cheek like narrow slashes of blood. "Just be careful, honey."

"Aren't I always?" he replied with a tender smile. He wondered how many men married for twenty-six years still lusted for their wives the way he did for his. "Sweet dreams," he whispered, kissing the soft, rounded flesh of her bare shoulder.

Judy didn't answer. That, too, was part of the game: she pretended to have fallen back to sleep and he feigned belief. She would, he knew, share her worries for his safety and sorrow about the tragedy over the next few days when they were alone together, but she would not burden him with them now, when he most needed to be clear-headed and alert. It was her way of supporting him, of giving him the freedom he needed to do his job well. He adored her for it.

Musuko padded behind him, bushy tail curled up over his back. At the front door Wilkes bent to stroke the short, rough reddish-brown back with a firm hand.

"No, boy," he said. "Just me, this time."

The heavy-set dog cocked his head. The pointed ears twitched. Wilkes could barely make out the dog's features, but the white blaze on his chest and his front paws gleamed in the darkness.

"Sit, Musuko. You stay and guard the girls."

The dog sat, obedient as always, the quivering of the powerful, stocky body attesting to his desire to accompany his master. Wilkes shut the door and strode to his six-year-old, dark gray Chrysler LeBaron. He would have liked to bring Musuko as he often did when called out late at night or early in the morning. But he knew that this time the commotion, especially since the media would probably get wind of this before Davisson's body could be removed, might upset the Japanese Akita's normally calm disposition. Not even Wilkes wanted to tangle with Musuko when the dog got riled.

Wilkes drove fast, ignoring stop signs and signal lights. He passed few cars on the streets. He kept to side roads, winding through the sleepy upper middle class area of the city where he lived, into the deteriorating poorer section. Fourth and Lexington was the center of a narrow no-man's-land six blocks wide and four miles long. It was a mixture of shops, warehouses, and single family homes a century or more old that separated the wealthy upper class from the reality of life on the firing line of drugs, crime and poverty. The area teetered on the fence, as it had for some years now. Neither rich nor poor nor middle-class, it defied designation, thumbed its nose at statistics. Tumbledown rat-traps interspersed with houses freshly painted. Vacant storefronts hobnobbed with successful, growing enterprises. Deserted warehouses stood beside converted loft apartments. Anything could come out of the Fourth and Lexington district, a big part of his precinct, and it often did.

The scene wasn't hard to find. Five blocks up from the river half a dozen police cars with lights flashing stood canted out into Fourth Street, blocking the alley entranceway. The meat wagon and a lab van blocked the Lexington Avenue access. Two patrol cars and one unmarked detective's vehicle flanked the crime scene in the alley itself. Wilkes studied the scene and found he couldn't fault the way this had been handled so far. No one, except the police and two civilians Wilkes assumed were the ones who had found the body, was anywhere near the corpse. Even the lab boys and a scowling medical examiner stood at a respectful distance. A few curious residents, awakened by the commotion and clutching sweaters over nightclothes, peered around police barricades and patrolmen. But his men had been busy. When and if the press did arrive—which would be soon, Wilkes was sure—there were enough barriers to ensure an un-compromised beginning to the investigation.

The body lay in a small cul-de-sac on the left, halfway down the one-way alley. A niche about ten feet deep had been sculpted into the surrounding brick building, a vacant pottery factory, creating somewhat of a courtyard effect. The original purpose of the niche was anybody's guess. Now the dark, secluded area, hemmed on three sides by windowless brick walls and faced by boarded windows in the storage warehouse across the alley, made a perfect meeting place for transactions of the unsavory sort. This was not the first body to be found here, and Ogden Wilkes knew it wouldn't be the last.

He parked, then edged around the unmarked whose headlights floodlit the crime scene. The car's owner, tall, beefy, lead homicide detective Bill Traynor, turned to intercept Wilkes as he approached the body. A uniformed patrolman stood nearby, just within earshot. Traynor's trainee, Andy Snelling, stood a few feet further away, hands and jaw clenched as he watched the grisly scene.

"Any problems, Bill? Wilkes asked.

Traynor opened his mouth, then closed it without speaking. Wilkes' eyes narrowed. After a beat,

Traynor's chin dipped once as though to reassure his Captain. Wilkes allowed himself to relax slightly.

"All's secure, sir," Traynor said, his hazel-green eyes glancing at the patrolmen guarding the Fourth Street entrance. "No one's been near him since I called you."

Wilkes nodded, then grimaced at the sound of tires screeching outside the alley. Slamming doors and shouting voices heralded the arrival of local news reporters.

"Goddamn, I knew it wouldn't last," he growled. "As if this isn't going to be difficult enough, now we have those fucking idiots to contend with. Well, we knew going in what it would be like, didn't we?"

He glanced at the detective. Traynor's lips twitched. Again his chin dipped in an abbreviated nod of agreement.

"The boys well-briefed?" Wilkes asked.

"Yes, sir." Traynor's eyes held a trace of amusement though his expression remained stern. "They'd keep the President out if you ordered it."

"I doubt it will come to that." Wilkes' chuckle held no mirth. "Davisson was big, but only in a pond this size." He stepped closer to where the body lay and turned to Snelling, his eyes narrowed on the young detective's face. "What's it look like to you?"

"Drugs, most likely, sir." Snelling swallowed obvious nervousness and took a deep breath. "Or organized crime. I'd say it was a pro job, all the way."

Wilkes grunted, pulled on latex gloves, and crouched beside the body, which lay on its side in the niche's rear corner closest to Fourth Street. The feisty, tenacious investigative reporter had taken quite a beating. Savage cuts marred his photogenic face. Blood matted his waving blond hair and stained the front of his white Italian silk shirt. His hands were bound behind his back, his blue eyes open, glassy and staring, the deep, resonant voice silenced forever. Snelling's high-pitched nasal tone showered down on Wilkes.

"Judging by the state of the body, sir, I'd say it took Davisson a long, hard time to die. That slug must have felt pretty good by the time they got around to it."

Wilkes nodded and rose.

"It certainly looks like someone with a grudge made damn sure Davisson got the message before driving the point home with a bullet."

Wilkes waved Bob Lesky closer. The M.E. waddled toward Wilkes.

"What would you say, Bob?" Wilkes gestured with his chin at the blood-ringed hole in Davisson's left temple. "A thirty-eight?"

"How the hell would I know?" Lesky's acerbic tone and sour expression confirmed his disagreeable disposition. "You think I have x-ray vision? When I go in, I'll know. I'll have it plated in silver and mounted like a trophy for your desk if you want. I'm not paid to make guesses. And I don't get out of bed at four a.m. so I can watch you prance around in the dark doing my job. You want to play games, fine." He turned away. "I'm going home. Wake me when it's over."

"Five more minutes, Bob, that's all. We can't afford a mistake on this one."

"What 'we'?" Lesky snarled as Wilkes again crouched beside Davisson. "Quit lumping me in with the rest of you clowns."

Wilkes chuckled absently as his gloved hands folded back the grimy, blood-encrusted suit coat. His fingers quested into pockets. He found keys, a wallet, three pieces of chewing gum and a white handkerchief with CDG monogrammed in blue in one corner. A silver Cross pen still peeked above the hem of the blood-stained shirt pocket. But there was no notebook, not one scrap of paper, not even a book of matches on which to write. Wilkes stood up and nodded at Lesky.

"He's all yours once the photog's done. ASAP, and don't leave one inch of him unexamined. I want to know everything that's happened to him since he was born."

"Oh, sure," Lesky wheezed as Wilkes turned away. "I won't bother to cut him, I'll just use a crystal ball, or better yet, my time machine." He pursed his thick lips and stood rocking on heels and toes while the lab men shot rolls of film.

Wilkes walked to the back wall of the niche and crouched where a pale tan epauletted raincoat, Davisson's 'trademark' in weather both sunny and foul, had been tossed. With careful fingers he examined it. Not a scrap of paper lurked in its deep pockets. The harsh light from the unmarked police car's headlamps made him squint when he looked up at his two detectives—Traynor, broad and muscular, with a prize fighter's face and his Italian mother's coloring; Snelling, red-haired and thin, with facial features more suited to a horse than a human. Good cops, both of them.

"Nothing," he said. "Not even his pocket recorder."

"Strange, that," Traynor said, his eyes skewing to Snelling and back to Wilkes. "For a reporter."

"Yeah. Isn't it?"

Wilkes rose and looked over to where television and newspaper reporters surged against police barricades. Television cameramen had added their lights to those of the detective's car. Telephoto lenses captured every movement. Boom mikes thrust forward like horizontal antennae. Wilkes knew he had to be careful about what he said, what was captured on film.

"This has to be connected with whatever Davisson was working on. Why else would they take all his notes, and the recorder? He had to have been onto something really big. Drugs or organized crime, you're probably right, Snelling." He looked at the detective and gestured at the crime scene techs. "I want every inch of this alley gone over. Tell them to print every goddamned brick if they have to. I want something to go on, fast."

"Sir," Snelling said, and marched down the alley to the knot of men scouring the cobbles where Davisson lay.

"I think we're going to need it, sir." Traynor's gravelly voice echoed slightly in the narrow space, his eyes scanning the press mob a short distance away. "One of their own has been killed. If those news hounds don't get acceptable answers, and get them fast, this is going to turn ugly."

"Shit!" Wilkes exclaimed as the thought hit him. Was it already too late? Reporters were nothing if not quick and clever. "Get someone over to the T.V. station, fast. Seal up his office. All we need is one of them getting to his files before we do. And his house, he must have kept some things there, too."

"It's already taken care of, sir." Traynor's flat voice rang in the enclosed space as Snelling returned to stand by his side. "Joe Sillitto's sitting on Davisson's office, checking through his paperwork. Won't nobody get inside 'til you OK it. And I sent patrolman Bates over to the house. Figured it wouldn't hurt to have a little protection already in place."

Wilkes' head turned in the dim light. He looked at Bill Traynor. The detective's eyes, still hooded and secretive, stared back. Wilkes nodded.

"Good thinking," he said and turned away to the bustling crime scene. Lab men worked on the ground around where Davisson had been found. Bob Lesky's assistants had already bagged the body and were lifting it into the coroner's van. Patrolman Abernathy stood beside his black-and-white talking with the young couple who had made the gruesome discovery. The woman sat sideways in the back seat, her feet out on the pavement, one hand clasped in her companion's. Abernathy's pen moved across his notebook. Anxious and angry camera crews and reporters milled at the Fourth Street barricade. Television cameras pointed in their direction. Wilkes had no doubt the mike booms could pick up his every word.

"Okay, Bill," he said, his quiet voice sounding almost menacing. "You and Snelling go help debrief the civilians. I'll run the press gauntlet. Then we'll move on this thing and we won't stop until we get the ones who did it. We'll start with Davisson's current stuff and work backwards if need be. I suppose it could be someone he nailed in the past." He turned and looked at the place where Cliff Davisson had died. "But I doubt it. It's someone current, and someone big. And we're going to nail him. We're going to nail him but good."

A Matter of Identity

CHAPTER ONE

I sat erect, motionless on the hard horsehair settee, facing Mr. Marlowe, a solicitor, I believe he is called. It was he who had just pronounced my doom, spelling out the 'myriad' options open to a penniless female left orphaned in the heart of London. In other words, I could hire out for service, go on the streets, or starve.

The room that had so intimidated me at first faded away. I was no longer aware of the aged oak paneling on the walls and ceiling that lent a musty air to the surroundings, the candled sconces burning without giving off much light. I barely saw the massive oak desk piled high with legal papers from among which he had taken what was left of my life, nor the leather-bound volumes which lined the walls. Despite the hushed atmosphere I felt like screaming, though I knew I was not capable of making a sound.

I stared at him in silence as his words sank in, hating him not only for what he had said, and would still say, but also for the supercilious air with which he said it. He reminded me of a ferret; thin to the point of emaciation and not over-tall, his dark hair slicked back like a shining cap. He wore a pearl gray sack coat of the latest, almost-lapelless style over an elaborate brocade waistcoat. The striped bow tie clasped round his neck looked as sharp and narrow as his face. His pointed nose seemed to sniff tragedy wherever he looked. Brown eyes bulged in their sockets, prying into my private feelings, and his pursed lips and nervous fingers gave the impression that he enjoyed destroying helpless females. Little did I know how right I was in that estimation.

"I don't understand," I said. "There is nothing at all? Surely, there must be—"

"I assure you, Miss Weston," he interrupted, his lips downturned at the fact that I dared question his pronouncement, "there is nothing at all. Upon your Father's demise, no more than 30 pounds were discovered on his person. After careful investigation, not one further asset has been uncovered."

He sat back in the embroidered armchair with a self-satisfied smirk. I looked down at the papers on the table between us, then back up at him.

"But," I began, but Mr. Marlowe would allow me no further opportunity for question or doubt. It was, after all, unseemly in a woman not to unconditionally accept a man's word.

"My dear young lady." His drawling tone rang with exasperated impatience. "I am well aware of the home you claim to own in Boston, Massachusetts."

Claim? My eyes widened at the implied insult to my honor.

"And," he continued, clearing his throat and adjusting his pince-nez with a delicate gesture, "I am also aware of the business interests into which your Father told you he had invested."

He paused and his look of melancholy pity froze the breath of protest in my throat. I knew then, with absolute certainty, that what I had most dreaded since my Father's suicide really was true. There was nothing left, neither here nor at home. Father's tales of partners in England, the need for a quick trip overseas to finalize important investments, the promise of shopping expeditions to replace clothing and items there hadn't been time to pack—all were lies. Lies! Disaster had finally overtaken him, and in true coward's style he had fled with me to England and then killed himself, leaving me penniless and alone with no way to return to America, and nothing there for me even if I could. Oh, Father!

I sat staring at Mr. Marlowe as I tried to force myself to breathe, to get my heart beating, my mind working. Only dimly did I hear his contempt-tinged words.

"I received Tuesday week a letter from a Mr. Alcott, in response to our enquiries. I believe he is your family solicitor—ahhh," he corrected himself, "attorney?"

He glanced at me for confirmation but I could

only lift my shoulders in ignorance. I knew nothing of any details of Father's finances.

"He has informed our office," here he removed a page from among the many on the table between us, "that all personal family holdings and possessions have been liquidated in order to pay debts incurred by one George Arnold Weston, Esquire."

At the mention of Father's name in connection with such scandal, shame washed over me and tears filled my eyes. I bowed my head, not wanting Mr. Marlowe's ferret-eyes to watch while I strove to bring my vision into focus. As I struggled, I listened to his dry, detached voice drone on.

"The monies realized from said liquidation have discharged all but a sum of just over eight thousand dollars." He shifted in his seat and made an odd sound low in his throat. "That is eight thousand *dollars*, Miss Weston, not pounds. I am afraid that, as your Father's only child and heir, his debts have now become yours. However, the international aspects of this case may somewhat alter the legal ramifications. Mr. Alcott and I are enquiring on your behalf."

The words expressed some hope, but his tone clearly indicated that, no matter what, I would, of course, bear complete responsibility for the repayment of the entire massive sum. How ironic, I thought, pressing a handkerchief to my misty eyes, that a woman could not have property or money of her own —indeed, she was owned herself by either father, brother or husband—yet she was responsible to repay the debts any of them incurred. But since gainful employment was beyond possibility for most women, just how was that repayment to be accomplished?

He had ceased speaking; the silence deafened me. I raised my head but I could not meet his eyes. Would I ever, I wondered, be able to meet anyone's eyes again? I felt trapped. My breath shortened and my head lightened as I turned my gaze to the window and the sky-blue promise of freedom glimpsed through it, a promise as false as all of Father's. What would become of me? How could I ever pay back such a vast sum of money? How would I even live from day to day?

Mr. Marlowe must have been touched by something in my plight, for he leaned forward and covered my tight-clasped hands with one of his own. Like his voice, his hand was soft but authoritative.

"I understand how difficult this must be for you, Miss Weston. Such a shock, coming on top of your Father's sudden.... ah.... demise. And for a gently bred lady, the situation in which you find yourself is quite difficult. There are so few options available."

He rose and paced about the room, crossing to his desk, to the window and back again to the chair placed opposite me in an endless round. I could do naught but follow him with my gaze, my mind in turmoil. What more would this day bring?

"Let me see, now," he said, "do you sew? Cook? Are you fluent in any foreign languages? Are you well-traveled? Do you paint? Sing? Can you play the piano? Do you play any instrument? What is your knowledge of geography?"

The questions flew at me, on and on, forever, it seemed to me, while I could only shake my head in negation, or whisper, "Some... a little... barely..." in answer. At last he stopped faced me and exploded in frustration.

"My word, Miss Weston, what *do* they teach young ladies in America?"

I could only stare at him, blinking back tears. How could I explain that Father did not approve of girls (me) learning or knowing anything other than basic reading and writing, and how to cater to a man's (his) whims? I most certainly could not tell Mr. Marlowe in which directions my skills lay, such as they were, for, excluding marriage, they equipped me only for the more disreputable of occupations. Another wonderful legacy from George Arnold Weston, Esq.

"I–I do have some knowledge of mathematics, Mr. Marlowe," I said at last. He merely stared at me, his opinion clear in his face. Knowledge of mathematics, indeed! Mathematics was a man's subject; no woman could possibly understand such things.

"Well," he sighed after a moment of silence, "we can *try* for governess, although I hold but little hope for success." He seated himself in the chair opposite me, once again taking charge of my life. "Aside from your obvious lack of accomplishments, you have no references and no one to speak for your character, which is more than imperative given the manner of your Father's death. Also, the fact that you are an American is certain to cause difficulties in all but the least-desirable posts. And," he added with a very definite note of disapproval in his tone, "you are much too lovely to be allowed near most wives' husbands."

The silence lengthened as we pondered his words. I felt hysteria begin to rise. Being pretty was what every girl hoped and prayed for. Father had often told me I 'would do', as did my own mirror, although I had not truly trusted my own judgment nor that of Father or his business associates. Now it seemed to me astoundingly comical that I should have clear, objective confirmation of beauty from one such as Mr. Marlowe, while being told that self-same beauty make me ineligible for gainful employment! Perhaps I was more suited for the streets; the idea of genteel starvation held no appeal for me at all.

He must have seen how close I was to the breaking point, for he rose, took my hands and helped me to my feet.

"Yes, yes," he said almost to himself, "most assuredly a companion post will do, if we could only find one. Indeed, yes. They are quite difficult to come by, you understand; most widows and elderly spinsters have a flock of poor relatives from which to choose. But surely there must be one or two who would consider taking you on. At reduced compensation, of course. After all, given your history," he shuddered a bit at his veiled reference to Father's suicide, "you could not expect the same wages as one with an impeccable background. A good selling point; yes, indeed, a very good selling point."

He steered me toward the door, patting my hands with what, I'm sure, he thought was a soothing gesture.

"Well, now, after my fees are paid, there should be enough for you to live on for two more weeks at the hotel, if you are frugal. Perhaps if we found you a small room, somewhere, we should not be so hard-pressed. Yes, yes... We shall see what can be done there, too."

Still speaking, he opened the door and handed me out before I could frame a reply, a comment, or a question, not that I was capable of speech at the moment.

"Just leave everything to me, Miss Weston. Something is sure to turn up, eventually." He turned to his clerk. "Please see that Miss Weston is returned safely to her hotel, Pickering. Good day, Miss Weston."

He gave me a slight bow and shut the office door in my face.

About the Author

Susan Tuttle, an award-winning writer, is a freelance editor, writing teacher and the slightly twisted author of the suspense novels *Tangled Webs, Sins of the Past, Proof of Identity, Piece By Piece* and *A Matter of Identity.* Short pieces appear in the SLO NightWriters anthology and anthologies from the Central Coast Chapter of Sisters in Crime (SinC).

Her critically acclaimed, 6-volume *Write It Right: Exercises to Unlock the Writer in Everyone* workbook series for fiction and creative nonfiction is based on her classes. Each workbook contains lessons and exercises for writers of all levels, in fiction and creative nonfiction.

Susan is past president of SLO NightWriters and the Central Coast Chapter of Sisters in Crime, and is presently the newsletter editor for both organizations. In her fiction life, she is working on two YA fantasy series, and a mystery series featuring her psychic detective, Skylark, who will debut in the short story "Murder Under the Oaks" in the upcoming SinC anthology, *Deadlines: Murder and Mayhem on the California Coast.* Look for two novellas to follow: *The Somewhen Murder* and *Dead Ringer.*

Susan is active in her church, where she is the head of the music ministry and works as the church's office manager. She also writes spiritual songs and is working on two different series of spiritual meditation books: *Lord, Let Me Walk: A Journey With Jesus Through Lent,* and *Lord, Let Me Walk: A Journey With Jesus Through The Parables.*

Susan lives on the Central Coast of California with her imaginary cat in a house filled with her (mostly unfinished) handmade quilts and (mostly finished) knitted scarves. Find her on LinkedIn, Facebook (susanwriter), Twitter (stuttlewriter), and follow her writing blog with its weekly writing prompts (Write Over the Hump) at www.SusanTuttleWrites.com.